ALL ACTIVITY IN ENGINEERING HAD CEASED. TORRES'S TEAM STOOD QUIETLY, WATCHING.

"Okay, Khala," said Torres. Her gaze was fastened on the hovering sphere. "Transport."

Khala touched the controls. The steady, pleasant hum the sphere had hitherto emitted turned into a screeching groan that assaulted the ears. The light grew bright, brighter, searing the retina, and Telek was forced to close his eyes even though he wanted to watch, wanted to see what would happen next.

This was surely the end. They had miscalculated, and this close to the dark matter, they'd all be dead within minutes. It would shatter the sphere, invade their bodies, phase them in and out of existence, and—

The hum ebbed. The light dimmed.

STAR TREK VOYAGER®

GHOST DANCE

DARK MATTERS

BOOK TWO OF THREE

CHRISTIE GOLDEN

POCKET BOOKS

New York   London   Toronto   Sydney   Singapore

An *Original* Publication of POCKET BOOKS

POCKET BOOKS, a division of Simon & Schuster, Inc.
1230 Avenue of the Americas, New York, NY 10020

This book is published by Pocket Books, a division of Simon & Schuster, Inc., under exclusive license from Paramount Pictures.

ISBN: 0-671-03583-5

First Pocket Books printing November 2000

10 9 8 7 6 5 4 3 2 1

POCKET and colophon are registered trademarks of Simon & Schuster, Inc.

Printed in the U.S.A.

This book is dedicated to the memory of
Mark Lenard

The noblest Romulan—and Vulcan—of them all

INTERLUDE

THE ENTITY HAD NO FORM, BUT IT COULD SEE, SMELL, taste, touch, hear, and sense. It had no mind, but it thought thoughts that went back to the very beginning of time, and dared reach forward to contemplate time's end. It was in all places and none, and in this place that was no place, it was content.

It drifted, thinking its vast thoughts and touching places in and out of time and space. Here, the Entity knew joy as it recalled something as simple, as unique, as an image of a beloved face. There, it tasted profound sorrow as an entire species blinked out of existence. It knew these emotions simultaneously and was in no way troubled by the conflicts. It simply drifted, dreaming.

The Entity was perhaps the single most powerful being in this or any universe, and it was as fragile as a spiderweb blown away by an errant wind.

It knew its complexities and contradictions, but always, the Entity had reveled in them alone.

Until now.

CHAPTER
1

THE SWEET, THICK SMOKE FROM THE BURNING LEAVES of the Sacred Plant wafted upward, wrapping the Culil in its gray embrace. Culil Matroci struggled not to cough, instead telling himself that the smoke was holy, it purified him, and it was only his weak, fleshly lungs attempting to resist the presence of the Divine.

If only he had the courage, as the Culil before him had, to lock himself into a closed room and let the holy smoke from the Sacred Plant fill up those fleshly lungs until he was entirely one with the spirit world. But Matroci was young, and sometimes the delights of the flesh were sweeter to him than the smoke of the Sacred Plant.

Sacrilege! his training screamed at him, and inwardly Matroci quailed at his lapse. Tonight, before he snatched what little sleep his position permitted, he would have to spend an extra session with the Sacred Plant smoke to purge himself of his blasphemy.

Still, he always kept a window open.

It was the Strangers who had done this to him, unsettled him so that he could not think with the peace and clarity that a Culil ought. It was not unusual for the Culilann to meet beings from other worlds, though it had seldom happened in Matroci's village of Sumar-ka. Was that not the first of the ninety-nine Chants? "Never think you are alone. The works of the Crafters are multitude, and little have you seen of them." Such encounters often proved mutually beneficial. Of course, that was after the Ordeal had been completed, something any representatives of a completely new race must undergo. This time, the Ordeal was proving to be precisely that, and Matroci could not find it in him to approve.

Despite his efforts, Matroci found himself thinking about them, even though this was supposed to be a time of deepest prayer and inward contemplation. His sanctuary, large and roomy to befit his august office, was decorated with furnishings of both grace and utility. Handcrafted, of course, to honor the Crafters. Only the Alilann artificially manufactured anything. Such unimaginative products were scorned by true Culilann, and the Culil would lose his office if he dared allow them in the sanctuary. So for the comfort of the Culil there were pillows and rugs upon which to recline, woven and sewn and stuffed by those who cared for the soft-furred *simli*, chairs crafted from the trunks of the Sacred Plant as well as other woods, bowls and cups spun on a turning wheel while clever fingers worked them into objects of almost unspeakable beauty. Beverages, pressed by steady tramping feet, filled those cups; fruits and vegetables harvested by free-hearted labor adorned the table, waiting to be consumed.

Sometimes, Matroci wondered why the Culil accepted such beautiful things when his position required him to mortify his flesh and shun such niceties. The dictates of the Crafters were sometimes rather confusing. On the one hand, it was clear in the writings that the Culil was not to take active pleasure in gifts. On the other, it was also written that the people were to honor the Culil with the labor of their hearts and hands, thus also honoring the Crafters. So Matroci was in the awkward position of having to accept gifts he was forbidden to truly use and enjoy.

He sometimes wished he were not so high ranking. He'd have fewer pretty things, but at least then he could appreciate them openly and honestly as the rest of the Culilann did.

The smoke was dissipating, thank the Crafters. His lungs still burned, but not quite so much as before. After a few more moments, the fire had consumed all the dried leaves, and there was only the faintest trace of their sweet scent clinging to Matroci's heavy robes and long, pale blue hair.

He prostrated himself in front of the altar, asked forgiveness for his wayward thoughts, and rose. He bathed his face with the herb-scented water and let it dry on his blue-hued skin. Droplets traced their way down his shaven chin and neck and past his high collar, and the cool dampness was annoying.

Trials, that's all every hour brought. More tests, more trials of his faith. Matroci wished he were not quite so young. It seemed that the Elders were much more entrenched in the faith than he was.

He rose, stretched, poured himself a cool drink from one of those beautifully wrought pitchers, and sipped the tangy beverage slowly. He tried not to think about how delicious it was, and how beautifully made was the goblet that held it.

There was a soft knock on his door. Matroci sighed and called, "Enter."

It was Trima, his Sa-Culil. She stood straight and tall, her long blue hair falling past her buttocks. Since the day she was pledged to the Crafters, Trima had never cut it. It was an old tradition, hardly followed much anymore. Matroci himself had been forced to cut his long locks a few turns ago when he'd gotten them hopelessly snarled, but as far as he knew, Trima had proudly let her hair grow longer and longer, untouched by shears if not by comb.

It was thick and glossy and quite beautiful, and not for the first time Matroci wondered what its heavy lengths would feel like between his fingers. But Trima was his responsibility, and he would no more act on his feelings than he would leap off the thatched roof thinking he could fly.

He placed his fingers first on his temples, then on his throat, then on his belly in the ritual threefold gesture that Trima always expected. She returned it in kind, executing the movements with exquisite grace.

"Greetings, Sa-Culil," said Matroci. "What is it you require of me? It is not time for your training sessions."

"No, good Culil." Her voice was as sweet as the bell that rang to call them all to prayer at sunrise. She paused for a moment and inhaled deeply, breathing what remained of the sacred smoke. *She never coughs,* Matroci thought sourly.

"I come from Soliss. He tells me that the Strangers are not healing well, despite the holy waters with which they have been anointed and the prayers we have said for them, even though they are—"

Her voice caught, and her eyes widened a little. Matroci felt for her then. Trima liked to project such an image of peace, of tranquility. She had been the one to find the Strangers, wandering bleeding on the holy ground, and the whole incident had clearly upset her. Their torn, broken bodies were nothing of peace and tranquility.

But the words of the Crafters were clear. These were Strangers of the most terrifying sort, utterly unknown, and the Culilann were not to provide any aid other than spiritual for a certain number of days. If they survived, then the Culilann would attend to their physical needs with all the hospitality the Crafters bade them show. If they died, then the Crafters had spoken.

Personally, Matroci didn't like it any better than Trima seemed to, but there wasn't much he could do. Soliss, the Minister of the small village, was the worst of all. It was in him to heal, and to sit by and watch anyone suffer, even Strangers as alien as these two, must be awful.

A thought came to him. "They must eat of the Sacred Fruit," he said.

Trima frowned primly, if such a thing were possible. "That is a rare sacrament, as you must surely know, Culil. Even we who are called to serve the Crafters do not partake other than at Midtime."

"We are bound to offer spiritual aid," said Matroci, standing up straighter. "Surely letting them partake of the Sacred Fruit is offering such aid."

"Yes, but—"

"Who is Culil, Trima?"

She colored at that, pale blue suffusing her soft, rounded cheeks. "You are, of course."

"You will do well to remember that," he said, with a harshness he did not feel. "Your tenure of trial is not yet over. Another could still take your place."

The color that had rushed to her pretty face now ebbed and her eyes opened wide in horror. Matroci regretted his words at once, but he had to admit, they had produced the desired effect. A Sa-Culil preoccupied with keeping her position was a Sa-Culil not inclined to challenge him. Normally, he did not mind her chastisements thinly disguised as innocent comments. He even enjoyed them. It kept him sharp, having so keen a student.

But the Strangers, the Strangers! It would seem that they were changing everything.

"Go and carry out my wishes, Sa-Culil Trima. See **to it th**at the Strangers have plenty of the fruit, that they may fill themselves with righteousness." *And fill starving, aching bellies with something that might help them survive,* he thought grimly.

Obediently Trima made the threefold gesture and backed out of his so-called radiant presence. She closed the two doors behind her, eyes on the floor.

Matroci stared at the door for some time after she had gone. Trima was right. He was playing with fire, twisting the words of the Crafters in such a way. Passing the fruit of the Sacred Plant off as spiritual aid was dangerously close to blasphemy. He bent his aching knees onto the soft pillow for another round of prayers.

There was silence from the pit. Soliss's gut wrenched as he approached. Perhaps they had fallen into an uneasy sleep at last, worn out with lack of food, of water, of care for their infected wounds. Blasphemous though he knew it to be, there were times when he despised the words of the Crafters, and never more than now.

He felt eyes upon him and knew that the rest of the village was watching his every move. Even though it was part of their faith that all had a calling and no one should be jealous of another, he knew that folk mistrusted his gift for healing. It skirted the line between the Culilann and the Alilann. His herbs smacked of artificially manufactured medicines, his knowledge of anatomy, of scientific curiosity and skill. Unlike the potters and weavers and artists, Ministers, as the Culilann called their healers, were the only ones with a counterpart in the Alilann caste.

And were, therefore, not to be trusted.

His visiting the Strangers so frequently was certain to be noted and commented upon, perhaps even to the Culil himself. Still, Soliss strode forward boldly, his head held high and his spine straight. Let them say what they would. He had to be true to himself.

He slowed as he approached the pit. Would that the long days of the Ordeal had passed and he could haul away the grate that covered it. As it was, he knelt beside the hole in the earth, shielded his eyes from the light of his planet's twin suns, and peered down.

The slighter one was asleep, his broken arm cradled protectively against his chest. Soliss did not know what the alien's race looked like when well, so the red spots on the cheeks that seemed almost gray could be normal. He doubted it. He did not need to be familiar with the Stranger's species to know fever when he saw it.

The other one, heavier of build, glanced up as Soliss's shadow fell across the grate. He, too, was injured, but appeared more hale than his compatriot. Still, the ragged tears in his abdomen wanted attention. Soliss felt a brief surge of fury that he was forbidden to give it.

"Greetings," he said.

"Good morning," said the Stranger with a hint of irony in his deep, smooth voice. "Lovely weather you have here on this planet. Glad it hasn't rained."

Soliss felt the moisture in the air and glanced up at the growing clouds. "It will," he said. "How is he?" he asked, nodding toward the sleeping Stranger.

"He's not well, as I know you know. His wound

is infected and the broken arm needs to be set before it starts trying to heal itself improperly." He turned his face back up to Soliss. In the bright morning light, Soliss could make out strange lines that were apparently painted on the being's left temple. "I wish you'd tell me your name. You're the only one who has come to see us. I'd like to address you properly."

Without realizing it, Soliss sat up straighter, unconsciously putting more distance between himself and the wounded Strangers.

"I am no one. You are Strangers. That is all we need to say to each other."

The alien stepped closer to the side of the pit. At the movement, his fellow woke up and groaned a little. "That's the worst coffee substitute you've come up with yet," he muttered, then lapsed into fevered slumber once more.

The dark-haired alien looked at him, then up again at Soliss.

"You wouldn't be coming here so often if you weren't concerned. Please, he needs help!"

Soliss rose and stepped away. The pleading of the Stranger was torment. He turned and almost collided with the small, lithe form of Trima. She was carrying a tray with some sort of fruit on it.

"Oh!" she gasped. Quickly Soliss reached out and steadied the tray. "Thank you."

Soliss looked at the fruit. He didn't recognize it. "Sa-Culil, what is this? Why have you brought this to me?"

She met his gaze evenly and with a hint of scorn.

"I bring the fruit of the Sacred Plant not for you, Soliss the Minister, but for the Strangers."

Soliss gaped. So, the lumpy green things on the tray were the fabled fruit of the Sacred Plant. They didn't look particularly appetizing.

"I have never seen these before," he said.

"Of course not. You are not a member of the religious order. Only we may partake of it."

The awe that Soliss felt evaporated in the face of Trima's snobbery. "Then why are you wasting it on Strangers?"

Trima looked displeased. "Culil Matroci orders it. He says that the holy writings order us to give spiritual aid to these Strangers, and that feeding them the Sacred Fruit is doing exactly that."

"But you don't agree?"

She didn't answer. She didn't have to. Frankly, Soliss could not care less if the Culil's decision sat well or ill with Trima. All he knew was that for the first time in days, these injured and perhaps dying aliens were permitted sustenance. He grabbed the fruits off the tray, ignoring Trima's indignant yelp, and knelt beside the grate.

The alien gazed up on him. "So you're Soliss the Minister," he said. His dark eyes fell upon the fruit. "Is that what I think it is?"

"It's the fruit of the Sacred Plant," Soliss said.

"It's food. I thought we weren't supposed to have food."

"It's spiritual ministering," Soliss said, a touch too forcefully. "You must eat it slowly, and think of holy things. It will please the Crafters." He didn't want to just toss the food in there. Seeing no alternative, Soliss lay down and pushed an arm through one of the grate's gaps.

"I will think of holy things," said the Stranger as he reached up to take the fruit, "but I can't guarantee I'll eat it slowly."

Their fingers brushed as the stranger took the fruit. Five fingers to a hand and an opposable thumb, just like Soliss's. His build was the same, the eyes, nose, and mouth in the same place. They were very much alike. It was unsettling.

Soliss handed down the rest of the fruit, then edged back and stood. The Stranger, despite his claim, didn't eat immediately. His dark-eyed gaze locked with Soliss's blue one.

"You are Soliss," he said again. "I have a name, too, as does my friend. The naming of a thing is powerful in my religious tradition."

"I do not wish to hear it," said Soliss, mindful of the disapproving presence of Trima only a few steps away.

"But I will say it, and then you will know. My name is Chakotay, and my companion is Tom Paris."

CHAPTER 2

CAPTAIN KATHRYN JANEWAY DIDN'T PARTICULARLY want breakfast, but her appearance in the mess hall at 0530 every morning over the last week had cheered the crew considerably. More than once, she'd spoken quietly to an exhausted B'Elanna Torres over a cup of Neelix's latest coffee substitute, or ruffled the auburn hair of little Naomi Wildman.

She'd chatted with Neelix himself, who kept apologizing for his attempted murder of their Romulan guest, and told him again and again that he had not been mentally capable of knowing what he was doing. Janeway thought the Talaxian was finally beginning to believe her.

She'd tried a fish-and-rice dish for breakfast that

Ensign Wu had sworn was divine, and found to her surprise that she liked it. And she had sat alone, knowing that even if no one chose to speak with her, her presence was seen and appreciated after the incredible and unsettling events of the last few weeks.

She, her crew, and the noble *Voyager* vessel that had gotten them this far had undergone a great deal together over the past six years. They had had their share of adventure, seen things both sublime and horrific, borne witness to some of the bravest, most compassionate acts living beings could commit as well as the most craven and appalling.

But the last couple of weeks had nearly eclipsed everything that had gone before.

She sipped her coffee substitute slowly. It was pretty good. A touch grainlike, but the aroma was damn near perfect.

It had begun with a series of mysterious wormholes that had apparently been following the ship. That led to the reunion with the Romulan scientist Telek R'Mor, who had told them a tale that seemed straight out of the realm of fiction. It was a story of dark matter and the aliens who manipulated it, of so-called Shepherds both benevolent and hostile. They had seen firsthand what this peculiar, mutated dark matter could inflict: murderous rage, paranoia, recurring nightmares, hallucinations, memory loss, cancers that wouldn't respond to treatment.

You name it, Janeway thought wryly, her mouth curving into a hint of a smile, *we had it.*

It had almost destroyed them and their ship, until they had managed to track down one of the kinder Shepherds, Tialin. She had appeared to them as an old woman and given them what B'Elanna Torres had taken to calling That Damned Ball. Inside That Damned Ball Tialin had placed all the dark matter that had been contaminating the ship. Right now, Torres, Telek, and Seven were hard at work trying to unlock the mystery of Shepherd technology as exemplified by the sphere. Once they understood it, they could put it to work and be about the surprising next phase of their journey. It was a good, old-fashioned quest in the cause of what was right. Tialin had asked them to take the orb and help the Shepherds track down and gather up the mutated dark matter still prevalent in the quadrant.

Janeway had agreed.

Her smile at the thought of herself as King Arthur leading the quest for the Holy Grail faded a little. Her best knight was not with her. There had been a price exacted, and even now Janeway didn't know how dear that price would eventually be. While on the planet, Commander Chakotay, her first officer and friend, and Ensign Tom Paris had disappeared.

Then, of course, there were the Romulans, and Khala. How they were going to make sense of all of this, Janeway had no clue.

Even as her thoughts turned to the young woman, Shamraa Khala Remilkansuur entered the mess hall with Harry Kim. People stopped in mid-chew, then hurriedly returned their attention to their meals. No one wanted to be rude, but Janeway knew her crew was desperately curious about Khala. She had been the only living thing on a dead planet, claiming to have no knowledge of how she had gotten there. That was a mystery, but nothing compared to the mystery Khala herself posed. The Doctor had run every test he could think of on their new guest, and it was beyond doubt. Khala was unlike any sentient creature with whom the Federation had ever come into contact.

She appeared humanoid enough, and beautiful at that: tall, slim, long, pale blue hair, blue eyes, opalescent blue skin. Save for her coloration, she could pass for human. But inside, things were "all wrong," as the Doctor put it. Her DNA sequencing was backward, and the very elements that comprised her seemed to be almost flip-flopped from standard humanoid development.

She stood hesitantly at the door, obviously very much aware of the interest she was generating simply by being present. Gently, Harry touched her shoulder and subtly urged her to step fully inside. Janeway was glad that Harry had taken such an interest in their guest. He was kind and humorous, and put Khala at ease.

Khala came to an abrupt stop in front of Neelix's kitchen area. She practically gaped.

"You . . . cook?" she said, with the faintest hint of disdain. Gingerly, as if it might explode in her hand, she reached to pick up a ripe red tomato. "You cook with *plants?*"

Neelix was in full regalia, from his apron to his

signature droopy chef's hat. "Indeed I do," he said, standing up to his full less-than-imposing height.

Khala turned to Harry. "But you told me about the replicators, how they functioned. I just had a cup of green tea in my quarters. I've had all my meals like that. That's how food is prepared, not like . . . like . . ." She broke off, her shock and distaste warring with her desire to be polite to the people who had shown her such care.

Janeway rose and moved swiftly, hoping to nip this cultural clash in the bud. "Good morning, Khala," she said. "I can't believe it's taken Harry this long to bring you to the mess hall. He's been remiss. There's nothing like a home-cooked meal."

"Captain, I am so sorry. Clearly I'm being rude." She straightened as if preparing to undergo torture. "Of course I'd love some . . . some cooked plants."

Neelix's annoyance was changing to compassion. "You poor child," he said. "Do you come from a place where there are no fresh foodstuffs?"

Immediately Janeway thought of war, of rationing. The Doctor had kept a close eye on Khala while completing his tests. It was only yesterday he had agreed to let her have free access to the ship. They hadn't had much chance to talk with her, learn about her very alien culture.

Khala blushed, her pale cheeks turning a deeper shade of blue. "Again, I apologize. On my planet, only the Culilann actually plant fruits and vegetables. They even raise living animals for slaughter. Can you imagine?"

Janeway thought of the occasional unreplicated leg of lamb she had enjoyed from time to time back on Earth. "Yes," she said, "I can imagine." She softened the words with an understanding smile and patted Khala gently on the arm. "And your people? What do they eat?"

"We are the Alilann. Many, many generations ago, we decided to embrace technology and science. The Culilann chose to forswear it. We can genetically engineer foods and supplements that are far superior in taste and nutritional value to anything that comes out of the ground."

Harry smiled a little. He reached over and with a raised eyebrow silently asked permission to borrow a knife. "Oh, please," said Neelix. Harry carefully cut the tomato into quarters and sprinkled it with a little salt.

"We grow the food in the aeroponics bay," he said. "No dirty soil there. And believe me, I think this tomato can beat a supplement for taste any day. This is how my father used to eat them—right out of the garden with just a sprinkle of salt. Try it."

He placed the quartered tomato to Khala's lips. For a second she pressed them shut tightly, then opened them and delicately took a small bite. Her eyes went wide with pleasure and her blue lips curved in a smile. Then, like a curtain descending, an expression of nausea passed over her features. She spat the half-masticated tomato into her palm.

"I am so sorry, I just . . . the thought of eating what the Culilann eat . . . I just can't do it."

"Don't worry, Khala," said Janeway at once. "It's no problem if you want to eat replicated food."

Her eyes lowered, Khala brushed off the offending piece of tomato onto a plate. "Captain, if this is how the crew eats, I don't want any special treatment."

"We eat fresh foods prepared by Neelix because we like them," said Harry. "We prefer real food to rations or even replicated food. But like the captain said, it's okay. Come on. We'll get you something to eat over here."

Again, the gentle hand on the arm, steering Khala away from her faux pas to the replicator. Janeway could no longer hear their conversation, but she didn't have to.

Neelix was silent, diligently cutting up fruit for juicing. "She meant no offense, Neelix," said Janeway.

"I know that," said Neelix. "I'm not angry. I just feel really sorry for her. Imagine not wanting this delicious tomato!"

Janeway stared at the red fruit. On impulse, she took a quarter, salted it, and popped it into her mouth. Neelix jokingly applauded her. Harry had been right. No replicated tomato could touch this for flavor and general sensuous satisfaction.

The ball floated serenely about five feet in the air, emanating a cool purple light, seemingly oblivious to their increasing frustration with it.

Seven of Nine was irritated. She was irritated with their lack of progress, with Lt. Torres's comments, with Telek R'Mor's slightly supercilious attitude. The team was a logical one, but a tense combination as well. They could not even seem to agree on which step needed to be taken first.

"Let us start again from the beginning," said Telek R'Mor, as calmly as if they had not already tried to start from the beginning at least four times. "Perhaps there is something we missed."

Seven stifled her irritation and inclined her head. Torres muttered something in Klingon, rolled her eyes, and folded her arms, but nodded anyway.

"We followed signs of Shepherd activity to the planet," said Telek. "When we reached the inside of the cave, we found a large floating sphere, like this," he nodded toward That Damned Ball. "It emanated a purple light. Commander Chakotay's tricorder indicated that there was some kind of energy located within the sphere itself that animated it." His dark eyes flickered from Seven to Torres. "I was not permitted to closely examine the cloaking apparatus given to us by Lhiau, but it was similar to this orb: small and beautiful, made of some sort of crystalline material. It pulsed with light."

"The light coming from That Damned Ball is steady," said Torres, almost nastily.

Telek stiffened, then said calmly, "I see the dark matter that has begun to permeate your system again is affecting your temper."

"Lieutenant Torres does not require mutated dark matter to display irascibility," said Seven. She felt a peculiar sense of pleasure at the scowl that furrowed Torres's face.

21

"It is immaterial," said Telek. "But since we have seen similar elements in three different pieces of Shepherd technology, it would be logical to assume that this is an integral part of all of their technology. When Captain Janeway touched the sphere in the cave, light poured forth from the orb. From within the sphere, or so it seemed, Tialin seemed to be . . . hatched."

"The orb in the cavern was most likely a form of teleportation device," said Seven, repeating the same conclusion they had reached a few hours ago. "The captain's manipulation of the orb sent a signal that Tialin's presence was desired, and she appeared."

"But it broke the orb," said Torres. "And we've handled That Damned Ball repeatedly and nothing's happened. It seems completely unbreakable."

"If we are to contain the dark matter within it," said Seven logically, "then we should be grateful that it is unbreakable."

Torres turned on Seven and was about to retort when Telek held up a hand. "Silence! A moment, please . . . let me think." Torres bit her lip and stayed silent, though the effort was clearly costing her.

Seven watched Telek, studying him. She had learned much from the Romulan about his way of thinking, of approaching problems. Cognitive analytical reasoning seemed to be a strength of his, and Seven, though not directly of the Borg Collective any longer, still had a deep instinct to take what she could from others and make herself the better for it.

Finally Telek stopped. "We've been going about this all wrong," he said.

"Oh, great," said Torres. "What do you mean?"

"We have been thinking that Tialin gave us the orb to contain the dark matter once we were able to extract it."

"Well, *she* put the dark matter in it," Torres replied.

"Yes, but perhaps only to show us something." Telek stepped forward and plucked the orb out of the air. It lay quietly in his palm. "I think she meant this as an example. What was it she said . . . I can't remember exactly."

"Your tricorder," said Seven suddenly. "If it was functioning properly, it should have recorded your entire encounter with Tialin."

"If the dark matter hasn't gotten to it first," muttered Torres, but she too looked more hopeful. She went to a console and called up the records. "It seems to be intact. Let's see what we've got."

They stepped back and watched the encounter with the Shepherd unfold.

"Only a few yards now," said the videorecorded voice of Telek. *"I don't understand why they're so still—they must be waiting to greet us formally."*

Telek scowled at the naïveté his recorded self displayed. *"Or kill us,"* said Janeway. *"We've got to be ready for that possibility."*

"The area opens up into a cavern," said Telek on the recording. *"Right around the corner."*

"Phasers at the ready," ordered the captain.

The three assembled in engineering watched the

soft, purple illumination flooding the cavern. Floating in the clearing, as its smaller cousin was doing right now in engineering, was the large sphere that was creating the light.

"It's humming," said Torres sharply. "This one isn't humming."

"Noted," said Seven, her eyes on the screen. She was pleased. Already, they had learned something. "Perhaps the sound indicates a level of activity."

"The apparatus Lhiau gave us also hummed when it was activated," said Telek.

The videorecording of Chakotay was speaking now. Seven felt a slight pain inside as she saw both Paris and Chakotay, who were missing now, alive and well on the recording.

"It's like no technology I've ever seen," Chakotay said. *"There's some kind of energy animating the sphere, coming from inside, but I don't know how to explain it. I can't even estimate its function."*

"Telek? Any thoughts?"

"This appears to be similar to the apparatus they gave us to manipulate dark matter. My method of tracking down the Shepherds was never exact, Captain. I knew how to look for signs of their activity. I incorrectly assumed that this signified their presence, not simply a piece of their technology. I apologize for our failure."

"It's ancient, that's for sure," said Chakotay. *"This sphere has been here for hundreds of thousands of years. Its energy is only detectable on the*

very narrow, precise band that Telek gave us. I'd say it's unlikely that the inhabitants of this planet were even aware it was here."

"The narrow band," said Seven. "The orb has been impervious to all attempts to scan it. Perhaps we should reconfigure the tricorders to this precise frequency."

Torres nodded, her excitement growing. "When we're done with this, we'll get on that right away."

Janeway stepped up to the orb in the cavern and placed her hand on it. The light increased. A shape appeared inside the orb. It curled and twined, but began to take on a definable form. The orb shattered.

A blond woman stepped out.

"Mother?" breathed Seven, her chest contracting. How could it be?

"B'Kor?" said B'Elanna at the same time. "Grandmother? What . . ."

"Tialin appeared differently to each of us, in the form of an elderly female we all knew and trusted," said Telek quickly. "I should have warned you."

The woman Seven saw was not elderly, but it was the only woman the child Annika had ever known. She steeled herself to watch and learn, and not be distracted by whatever form Tialin the Shepherd chose to assume.

"I am Tialin of the Shepherds," said Annika's mother. *"You need my help—and we need yours."*

"I don't understand," said Janeway. *"You need our help?"*

Tialin sighed. *"I suppose after your encounter with Lhiau I can understand your suspicion."*

"You bet," muttered Torres.

"I don't have time for this," snapped Janeway, stepping forward. Her hands went to her hips. *"Are you a member of the Q continuum? You're certainly behaving like one."*

"Oh God," said Torres over the captain's next comment. "I hadn't even *thought* of that."

"Ah, the Q," Tialin said. *"Most amusing. Tricky folk, though, don't you find?"*

"No trickier than you," said the videorecording of Telek. *"We are dying. My people back in the Alpha Quadrant are dying, and all because of Shepherd—"*

Looking uncomfortable, Telek stepped forward and pressed the keypads. The recorded image sped forward. "There is nothing here about the orb," he said by way of explanation. "Tialin explained that Lhiau was a rogue. This was when she removed the dark matter. There is absolutely no physical indication of how it was done. Here. This is where the sphere appears."

"Gaze into the sphere," said Tialin. *"See there, caught safely, the First Things which have so plagued you. We have removed every trace of altered dark matter from your bodies and your vessels, and have contained it all within this sphere. I have rendered it visible to your limited range of viewing. It will trouble you and your crew no longer."*

"See? She put it in That Damned Ball," said Torres.

"But think, Lieutenant. The sphere contains all the dark matter from our bodies and the ship, yes. But Tialin later indicates that there's much more out there.

How can this small orb contain so much dark matter? It must be an example, not the final container."

"Dark matter is very tiny," Torres pointed out.

"So is a drop of water," said Telek. "But an ocean is a very large thing indeed."

Seven gazed at the levitating orb. "Perhaps there is more to this sphere than we think." She was anxious to begin examining it on the precise frequency Telek had used before and was impatient with the recording. Nonetheless, it had proved useful already. There might yet be more to learn from it.

On the video, Tialin was tossing the ball to Paris. Torres's expression sobered somewhat. They listened in silence as Tialin explained that dark matter existed simultaneously in all universes, completely in none, save when it came into contact with subspace. This was what the evil Lhiau was doing: pulling the dark matter completely into the universe, rendering it incredibly dangerous. She asked for *Voyager*'s help in tracking down the rest of the mutated dark matter.

"Here it is," said Telek.

"We gift this technology to you," Tialin said.

"Yes," said Torres, "I know that, but . . ."

"Shh," said Telek. "Listen."

"We will give you the ability to locate and contain the mutated dark matter," continued Tialin.

"We know how to locate it," said Telek. "We've already reconfigured the transporters. The orb is the key to telling us how to contain it."

Torres had opened her mouth when the scream startled them all. It had come from the tricorder recording, and it had issued from Khala's throat. They stared, transfixed and silent, as light flooded the cavern.

"No!" Khala was crying. "No, not again, not to another dead place—"

Seven recognized that light. It was the same brilliant illumination they had seen just before an entire planet winked out of existence, only to return devastated. Rocks seemed to appear from nowhere, and Paris was in their path. Chakotay dove for Tom and knocked him out of harm's way. Dust rose up, but they were all right. Chakotay looked at the light, at Khala, at his captain, then seized Paris and ran with him toward the heart of the light. He disappeared from view. They were gone.

"The captain was correct," said Seven. "Commander Chakotay obviously chose to enter the portal, and to take Ensign Paris with him."

"Cold comfort," said B'Elanna, almost too softly to hear. Seven said nothing.

Telek stepped forward and turned off the recording. "There is nothing further about the dark matter. Lieutenant, I believe it is obvious. Tialin thought to teach us by example. The amount of dark matter that was in this ship and its crew, which is now contained within the sphere, is infinitesimal compared to the amount that is still out there. Since I was not under the impression that she planned to drop by now and then to empty the orb for us, I suggest we begin working on how to create something similar of our own."

Seven narrowed her eyes. It was the first time she had seen Telek display humor.

"Oh," said Torres. "Well, when you put it that

way, it sounds so simple. Let's get on it and we'll be done in time for lunch."

Seven was about to reply when she realized that Torres was utilizing a form of speech called sarcasm. She kept her mouth closed and regarded the floating orb, which still kept its secrets. For the first time, Seven of Nine understood why *Voyager*'s chief engineer insisted on referring to it as That Damned Ball.

CHAPTER

3

JEKRI KALEH, THE "LITTLE DAGGER," CHAIRMAN OF the Romulan intelligence service the Tal Shiar, stood rigidly at attention on the left side of her Empress. All eyes were fixed on the viewscreen that occupied a full wall of the Senate Chamber.

No one spoke, though Jekri knew that on this black day hearts were breaking and careers were crumbling. There, on the screen, was the only remaining warbird to have survived the encounter with the Federation starship *Voyager* in the Delta Quadrant.

It was difficult for even Jekri, who held few ideals, to believe their project had come to this. It had been years in the planning. When Telek R'Mor had returned from his trip to the Delta Quadrant after having actually stepped aboard *Voyager,* Jekri had been waiting for him. He had been pressed into service, his fine mind and keen intellect put to the task of working for the Tal Shiar, along with the stranger, Ambassador Lhiau.

Lhiau. It was a struggle to keep the hated name from blazing in her brain. Even as Jekri dragged her thoughts back to the viewscreen, she saw Lhiau turn and look at her briefly.

He had come with an offer that had seemed too good to be true. He would give the Romulans cloaks made of dark matter which would render them utterly undetectable. In exchange, he wanted Romulan aid against some vaguely described "enemies."

It had seemed so simple, so straightforward so . . . Romulan. They would place Lhiau's cloaks on thirteen warbirds and use Telek R'Mor's wormhole technology to accomplish their goal: enter the Delta Quadrant, capture *Voyager,* and bring her back to be the new Romulan flagship in a total, crushing war against the Federation.

But that wasn't what had happened.

What had happened was that either R'Mor had deserted or the Federation had kidnapped him. What had happened was that when they finally again located *Voyager* and sent their so-wonderfully-cloaked warbirds after her, the Federation vessel had destroyed all but one. What had happened was that one remaining warbird was left practically disintegrating before their eyes.

And now, with a single word, the Empress was about to complete that process.

Jekri began to fidget, just a little. When would the Empress give her command? All the crew aboard the ill-fated vessel had already succumbed to some strange sickness that ravaged their bodies and minds. This empty hull was all that was left. It was past time to consign it to its fate.

The Empress licked her lips and cleared her throat. "Now," was all she said.

The screen exploded in white light that burned its way onto their retinas for a moment. When they could see again, small pieces of drifting wreckage were all that remained to mark where one of the mightiest vessels in the Romulan fleet had been.

"This is your doing, Little Dagger," said the Empress.

Startled, Jekri turned. "My doing, Excellency?"

"Yours," repeated the Empress. "This project has been under your auspices for the last several years. It was you who permitted Telek R'Mor to escape. You did not foresee what his wormholes would do to our mighty warbirds."

Jekri did not even try to defend herself, though outrage flooded every cell. She stood even taller, taking the undeserved tongue-lashing the Empress for some strange reason saw fit to dole out in front of the entire Senate. She listened only with half an ear to the accusations of sloth, of carelessness, of not knowing things she had no way of knowing.

Finally, like an ancient toy whose key has finished its revolutions, the Empress wound down. She pressed a slim, elegant hand to her temple for a moment and closed her eyes.

She was obviously on edge. They all were. Jekri had been a target for a frustrated, alarmed young leader, that was all. Jekri hoped that if she could recognize it, the others assembled would as well.

After a long, awkward moment, the Empress raised her head. "So the last warbird that went against the Federation *Starship Voyager* has been consigned to the emptiness of space," she said. "Those who crewed the ships are all either dying or dead. I will not cast a false sheen of some token glory over this terrible incident. We lost, and we lost badly."

She rose to her full graceful height. There was a scraping sound of chairs being pushed back as the seated Senate rose with her.

"This must not happen again. We must investigate what went wrong and see to it that it does not recur. Ambassador Lhiau has offered his knowledge, which exceeds ours in such matters. Like the ancient Earth creature the phoenix, we will rise from these dark ashes to our eventual triumph. Lhiau, attend me."

She swept from the hall in a shimmer of blue gossamer material, striding down the long stone hallway with her proud head held high. Lhiau followed her at a respectful distance.

Jekri watched them go with narrowed eyes. She was not sure whether to be happy or regretful that the unfathomable yet utterly untrustworthy ambassador had chosen to cleave unto the Empress instead of the chairman of the Tal Shiar. She despised him and was glad of his absence, but wondered why he had taken this sudden interest in the Empress. She was beautiful and powerful. Could it simply be that?

Jekri didn't think that Lhiau would be involved with anything simple.

The silence was profound. Jekri almost laughed. The Empress had never before risen and left in such an abrupt fashion, and all these senators didn't know what to do under the circumstances.

She glanced at the Praetor and lifted an eyebrow. He nodded slightly.

"This assemblage is dismissed," he said in his high, too-frail voice. "Long live the Empress!"

Everyone present saluted the absent Empress and repeated, "Long live the Empress!"

"Long live the Empire!"

"Long live the Empire!" Now the hall, which had been so still a moment ago, was alive with murmurs and echoes as the Senate began to disperse.

As Jekri began to stride down the hall, intent on returning to her own ship, the *Tektral,* to begin another set of hushed meetings with her second, Subcommander Verrak, the Praetor stopped her.

"I admired your restraint, Chairman," he said. "The Empress's words were unfounded."

"Thank you, Praetor," said Jekri. She again started to leave, a touch impatient.

"Although," continued the Praetor, matching her stride for stride as they walked down the enormous corridor, the colorful banners of every noble Romulan house hanging above their heads, "she did raise some interesting questions."

Jekri's heart lurched. "How so?" She flashed her keen silver eyes at him, wondering what he knew, and from whom he had learned it.

"It is indeed unfortunate that Telek R'Mor was able to escape to *Voyager.*"

"You speak of nothing I do not already know," Jekri retorted. "I have heard the most vigorous condemnation for that. There is much I would give to have the traitor safely in my grip at the present moment. Personally, it would make things easier for me and my people. Surely you must know that."

Yes, she thought, filling her mind with the images, *he is a traitor. He was not abducted against his will. No, he chose to leave, and we did all we could to catch him.* It was important that the thoughts feel utterly solid and sincere. Jekri suspected someone might be listening.

The Praetor nodded. "So it appears."

Jekri halted abruptly, her temper rising. "I cannot speak against my Empress," she said, "but you are not my royal leader. I grow weary of this subtle war of words. At least the Empress says what she thinks. What do you think, Praetor? What does the Proconsul think, and the Senate? Pray, tell me to my face!"

"Odd words, coming from the Chairman of the Tal Shiar," hissed the Praetor, his color rising. "From the Little Dagger who lurks in the shadows."

Jekri lifted a hand, ready to strike against this challenge to her hard-won honor. Only the Praetor and the Empress could call her by her former nickname, Little Dagger. She could not challenge the Empress, her sworn liege, but she was tense and nervous, and the Praetor was a colleague, not a queen. The Praetor was swifter. His fingers clamped down on her wrist. She would have bruises there in an hour. At once he let go and glanced about. Several people had seen them, and were still watching.

"I think to warn you, *veruul*," he hissed. "What are you doing, attempting to strike me in public in such a fashion?"

"What are you doing, all but accusing me in public in such a fashion?"

He ignored her and began walking again. She followed, her breath coming quickly.

"I think you were very unlucky in R'Mor's escape," the Praetor said softly. "I think Lhiau dislikes you, and I think it is mutual. I think you may have overlooked something, and I think you need to get back into the Empress's good graces very, very quickly. And I think, Little Dagger, that you need to watch your back."

It was good to be aboard her own ship, with crew members she knew with reasonable certainty to be loyal to her. Jekri returned the salute the transporter operator gave her.

"Welcome back, Honored Chairman," said the young man.

"Thank you. I will be in my quarters. Tell Subcommander Verrak to meet me there."

Out of the corner of her eye, Jekri noticed a slight smile on the lips of the transporter operator at her last words. Everyone aboard the *Tektral* thought that she and Verrak were having an affair. They had been just unsubtle enough about it to make sure the rumors flew. For a moment, Jekri felt a surge of irritation. Did her own crew think so little of her ability to keep a secret that they truly believed she'd let anything slip if she and Verrak were actually involved?

Apparently so. It annoyed her.

She strode down the halls, nodding to her crew, and entered her private quarters with a sigh of relief.

Many high-ranking officials filled their quarters with items from their past. There was a sentimental streak in the Romulan nature—exhibited by Telek R'Mor, for example—that often prompted otherwise focused individuals to have holophotos of family and friends in their rooms. More understandable, to Jekri, was the penchant for trophies: pieces of an enemy battleship that had been destroyed by a mighty warbird, an artifact collected as tribute from a new world that had joined the Empire, medals and commendations and art.

Jekri's quarters were all but bare. Of her past, she wished no reminders. Even if she had possessed anything at all, who would desire being constantly reminded of a brutal, harsh, hand-to-mouth existence in the poorest province on the planet? As for war trophies, she had none to display. She had won the occasional medal or two, but they meant little to her and, save for when they were required wearing at formal occasions, they sat out of sight in a drawer.

Anyway, she didn't spend much time in her quarters. Unlike some of her predecessors, Jekri was not content to sit quietly in the shadows and manipulate. She moved among the shadows herself, though less often than she had in past years. She liked to be where the troublemakers were, and that was everywhere in the Empire. Quarters were for occasional periods of respite.

The door hissed open and Verrak entered.

"Were you seen?"

"By one or two," he answered. "I almost literally ran into Sharibor." They both smiled a little; Sharibor Krel was known for her clumsiness.

"Good," Jekri replied. It would keep up the illusion of an illicit tryst. There was only one chair in the room. Verrak took it while Jekri seated herself on the bed. She anticipated there was going to be a lot of activity in this room over the next hour, but none of it would be physical.

"With your permission, Chairman," Verrak began, "I could not help but observe that you had words with the Praetor after the meeting."

Jekri scowled. "You and far too many other, less friendly eyes witnessed that. Yes, we had words. I do think he shares our dislike of . . . of him."

Ever since Jekri had discovered that Lhiau could read thoughts, she and Verrak had agreed to refer to him in private merely as "him." Surely the utterance of the being's name risked attracting unwanted attention. For the same reason, they had feigned this affair. If Lhiau thought they were coupling like *hnoiyikar* when they paired off and sought privacy, he was less likely to eavesdrop on their thoughts. She detected contempt from him as well. So much the better. One does not pay much attention to something one believes is beneath one's dignity.

Her only regret was that she had played upon Verrak's known, but unspoken, feelings for her. For that she was sorry, but the higher need drove her.

"Everyone shares our dislike of him," said Verrak.

Jekri leaned back, thinking. "Not everyone. Do you recall his treatment of our Empress? When he first came, he was as rude to her as he was to all of us. But at the last several Senate gatherings, he has been all concern and compassion for the tragic deaths of our people. I trust *that* less than I trusted his contempt. He also has not contacted us as much as he did in the beginning. He has done with us, Verrak, which could be a good thing. But he has not done with the Empress."

Her silver eyes gazed at the ceiling of her quarters, but she did not see its flat, cool blue surface. She saw a weeping Empress, young and vulnerable, and a calculating alien who would take his chance where he could.

"No, Verrak. He has not done with her at all."

INTERLUDE

HOW LONG HAD THE ENTITY BEEN DRIFTING? SECONDS? Centuries? It did not know. It was beyond the confines of the thing called time, and merely was.

Gradually, oh so gradually, it became aware of another presence besides itself. Curiosity stirred, a familiar sensation, though one not experienced for some time. It sent out its curiosity, and was answered.

We know what you are. The words came without voice or even sound, permeating the Entity's consciousness. That amused it a little. Amusement. Another sensation with which it had once been familiar. Interesting. It was amused because it itself had no idea what it was. It thought this.

You will soon find out, reassured the other Pres-

ence. We can aid you in that quest, if you will aid us in ours.

Quest. Not a task, not a job, not an errand or assistance. A quest. A noble term. The Entity understood nobility. It wondered what this quest might be.

The other Presence now seemed to hesitate, then it conveyed its intentions and reasons without words.

An anger, a rage so intense it could not be contained. A hatred of things the way they were and a desire to bring about change. Any change. At any cost. Lies. Deceit. Manipulation and greed and a burning desire for conquest. Pain. Pain! Though the Entity had no corporeal body, it writhed with the agony of the images presented by the Presence. Fear, washing over the Entity like something tangible. Death. Destruction.

The end of things.

The end of everything.

The Entity was in torment, wondering what it could possibly do to stop so great an evil with so vast a reach.

At once the images changed. The Entity was made aware of planet systems, of sentient beings, of vast clusters of something that was once natural and harmless turned into an instrument of destruction.

It understood what the Presence wanted, and why it wanted it. And the Entity agreed to lend its aid.

CHAPTER 4

"YOU'RE AN INTERCEPTOR, SHAMRAA EZBAI REMILKAN-suur," growled the Implementer. "That means you are supposed to *intercept*."

Ezbai's face was expressionless. "I understand the duties of my position, sir."

"Apparently, you do not. What were you doing while two alien life-forms manifested in Culilann territory? Puttering in the garden? Painting a picture?" Scorn dripped from the Implementer's words. His face was flushed deep blue with rage. For a brief, angry moment, Ezbai hoped he'd have a seizure and keel over. Anything to stop this so-called interview that was actually more of a mental torture session.

Ezbai and his whole family had, in fact, been otherwise engaged at the time when the aliens had appeared. His sister Khala had been seated at the table on one of her rare visits home when a strange light had exploded from nowhere. By the time they could see again, Khala had vanished.

He had reported it at once, of course. Within moments, teams had arrived at the domicile, sweeping with information recorders, taking gauges of radiation, looking for any signs of alien intervention. They had found nothing. Khala had been there, and then she had not.

They buzzed about abductions, transportation devices, off-world kidnappers who looked for slaves to trade. Ezbai had done what pathetically little he could to calm his wild, grief-stricken, elderly parents. The teams sent by the Order did nothing to help. There had been the insistent chirping of his communications console, but he had ignored it. He found out only when he entered this office ten clicks ago that it had been an alien intruder alert in Section 40329—Ezbai's section. And Ezbai was an interceptor.

And now here was the head of the Order, the fat and rude Implementer, calling him a *gardener* or a *painter*. Ezbai's attention had lapsed, perhaps, but surely the circumstances were understandable. There was no need for such insults.

"You know very well what I was occupied with at that time, Implementer." Ezbai's voice was carefully controlled. "My sister disappeared, and—"

"And there were teams taking care of the incident," retorted the Implementer. Standing on his feet and raging at Ezbai was exhausting him, so he sank back into his chair and popped an articrunch into his mouth. His jowls shook as he chewed. Ezbai fought the urge to leap up and throttle his superior. He consoled himself with the knowledge that his fingers probably couldn't tighten sufficiently around the thick neck to do the job.

"They were going about their business, Shamraa Ezbai. You should have been about yours. Do you know that by this time the aliens are well into the Ordeal? Barbaric custom, that. Makes my skin prickle just to think about it. No food, no water, just prayers." He shuddered and reached for a fistful of the artificially manufactured crispy treats. "They're lucky to be alive."

That last line revived Ezbai. "They're still alive? Your report said that they were gravely injured."

The Implementer frowned. "What did I just say? Our spy reports that they are still alive, though of course the Culilann haven't done anything to dress their wounds. The Culil authorized feeding the aliens fruit from their Holy Tree."

"Sacred Plant," Ezbai corrected absently. His mind was racing. If they were alive, they could be gotten out. To a degree, the obese Implementer was right. Ezbai was the interceptor in charge of the section in question. Within minutes of getting the notification, he should have had a team out there scouting the area to get to the aliens before the Culilann did.

The report certainly was intriguing. A new race that had seemingly appeared on the planet without detection. No ship in orbit, no energy residue detectable. It was as if they'd just manifested, like something out of a primitive Culilann folktale. Still, even if Ezbai hadn't been otherwise engaged, he would have been hard-pressed to locate and intercept the aliens in time. Normally, an interceptor's job was nothing so exciting as tracking aliens on the planet on foot. They picked up communications, or noticed ships approaching the planet. There was an excellent communications system in place among the Alilann, and it had seldom failed.

Always a first time, he thought. Then what the Implementer had just said fully registered. Ezbai sat upright and repeated, "The Culil authorized feeding them the fruit of the Sacred Plant?"

The Implementer scowled. "That's the second time you've asked me to repeat myself. Should you see the doctor and have your hearing checked?"

"But . . . that's unheard of!" Ezbai sputtered. "No one save the religious order ever partakes of the fruit of the Sacred Plant. What is the Culil trying to do?"

"Our spy was as puzzled as we were," said the Implementer with a full mouth. Crumbs of articrunch flew from his lips as he spoke. "There may be more sympathy with us than we had previously imagined."

"That would be all to the good, if it were true. Will the Silent One be able to assist us once the aliens are released from the ordeal?"

"Negative. We do not wish to risk exposing our sources."

Ezbai sighed. It would make things so much easier, but he understood the Implementer's reasoning. This particular spy, who went by the code name Silent One, had been planted years ago. The story was unassailable. They'd never had anyone planted so deep, in such an important position, in any of the sections before. There was very little that would justify exposing the Silent One, and these two aliens, intriguing though they were, weren't reason enough.

He would have to send in a recovery team. On the spur of the moment, Ezbai decided that he would lead them. He had the training and the authority, although it was a long time since he had practiced simulation runs as part of his training. It would help get his mind off Khala. Besides, it would be fun.

Ezbai sat up straighter. "All right. Here is my strategy."

The night that it rained, Chakotay and Tom stood beneath the grates with open mouths.

At first the rain, thick with mud and chalky tasting, cooled their fevered bodies and felt wonderful. After a few moments, though, they both started to shiver as their uniforms got soaked and their skin temperatures dropped. Still, they stood, mouths open, parched tongues seeking any kind of moisture.

Chakotay had a fleeting moment of black humor as he realized that, to anyone observing them, they would resemble nothing so much as baby birds waiting for Mama to stuff worms into their mouths. He thought about relaying the humorous image to Tom, but decided against it. Tom was very ill and even his famous wry wit had dissipated under the days of torment they'd been forced to endure.

Chakotay swallowed a mouthful of muddy water. His stomach roiled. It was now two days since they'd devoured the bitter-tasting fruit of the apparently sacred tree, and his belly was utterly empty. It wanted pure, cool water, a sip at a time, and some dry toast to ease it back to normal functioning. What it did not want, but he knew his body needed, was this foul, sludgy mess that passed for rainwater. He clenched his teeth against the rising gorge. He needed it, every bit of moisture, and he'd be damned if he'd vomit it away.

Tom doubled over, clearly having the same battle as Chakotay had with his sullen, shrunken stomach. He, too, managed to keep the water down. For now.

Paris was in bad shape. Chakotay had employed all his field training to dress their wounds, but without even water to cleanse away dirt or bandages to protect them, his efforts had been of little help. He knew the lacerations on his own stomach were infected. In darker, more exhausted moments, he fancied he could even smell the sweet, sickly stench of gangrene. Tom's arm was definitely in bad shape. There was nothing, not even twigs, to hold the set Chakotay had tried to give it on their first day here. Tom's screams of agony still rang in his ears. He had not tried again. There was no point in simply tormenting Paris.

They had come through whatever portal it was that they had entered when Chakotay, pulling Tom with him, had leaped into the light. Chakotay had had no sensation of movement at all. When the light faded, they were standing in a grassy meadow on the edge of a rain forest, blinking at the illumination of not some fey, incomprehensible light, but the simple pure radiance of twin suns.

"What happened?" Tom had asked, looking around and blinking.

"I'm not sure," said Chakotay. He tapped his combadge. It chirped reassuringly. "The combadges still work, at least. We'll be able to talk with anyone we encounter." He looked at Tom. "And get you some medical attention."

"You too," Paris replied, his gaze on Chakotay's torn belly. "That is, if there are any inhabitants here."

Chakotay's gaze fell upon a white building in the distance. It gleamed in the light, a beautiful contrast to the azure sky. "I'd say there are inhabitants. Let's go."

They began walking toward the large white building. Soft blue-green grass yielded beneath their boots. "Chakotay, what is going on? Why did you haul me with you through that portal?"

Chakotay didn't answer at once. "I'm not sure I understand it completely myself. When the light manifested in the cavern and the boulders fell through, I realized that they would weigh about as much as I did. Two of them would equal two human males. Khala started screaming that this was exactly what happened when she had been pulled to the planet against her will, and I made some kind of connection."

He shook his head. Sweat began to gleam on his brow. With two suns, this was a warm planet. It was clearly tropical as well, if the level of humidity was any indication.

"Once, the light appeared and Khala came through. It appeared again, and boulders came through. It somehow made sense that we had to go to the place where the boulders came from, to keep the balance."

"Pretty wild idea, don't you think?"

Chakotay frowned. "It seems like it now, but at the moment—Tom, somehow I knew it was right. I didn't even have a chance to explain it to the captain, or you."

"Why me?" Paris smiled a little. "Does this strange place you've dragged us to require a dashing blond ensign?"

"If so, I'd have brought along Ensign Jenkins. She's pretty dashing." They exchanged grins, then Chakotay sobered. "Sorry, Tom, you were just the closest body."

"Yeah, I got that a lot at the Academy." The joking over, he asked, "Okay, I believe in hunches, and let's say this was a good one. The fact remains that we don't know where the hell we are, or how to get back to *Voyager.*"

Chakotay didn't answer. He had no answers to give.

They walked on, the beautiful building growing closer. A shrill voice stopped them in their tracks.

"Halt! You are trespassing on sacred ground!"

They turned to see a beautiful young woman dressed in flowing robes of gray and blue. Her long, pale blue hair fell almost to the grass and was unbound. The wind played with it. Chakotay thought her one of the most beautiful women he'd ever seen, except for the icy expression of hauteur on her lovely blue-skinned features. Her fingers gripped a basket full of what seemed to be herbs.

"Please forgive us," said Chakotay. "We did not realize we were trespassing on your holy place." As he spoke, he was sizing her up. She was obviously from Khala's race, but there was no indication on her person that she was from an advanced civilization: no communication devices, no weapons that he could see. Nothing about the building—temple of some sort, he now supposed it to be—gave any hint that this was a post-warp-technology civilization. Until they knew for certain, the Prime Directive would have to be in full force. Khala might be from an advanced civilization, but not every cluster of people on every planet progressed at the same pace.

The woman's eyes narrowed. "You are wounded."

"Yes. We require attention, especially my friend. His arm is broken. Is there a . . . a healer among you?"

The woman gathered the basket closer to her, putting up a barrier between herself and them. "You are Strangers, of a sort with which we are unfamiliar. How did you get here?"

"It's a very long story," said Paris before Chakotay could interrupt. He smiled, charmingly. "Please . . . could you help us?"

The woman straightened. "You are Strangers," she repeated. "I am not permitted to interact with you. I have already done too much and will need to be purged of my transgression. Wait here. I will send someone."

Without another word, she turned and strode toward the building. They watched her go.

"Friendly sort," said Paris. "Makes Khala seem positively gushy."

"Yes," said Chakotay, not really paying attention. "She is definitely of Khala's species."

"Do we wait?"

"Unless you want me to set that broken arm myself, we wait," said Chakotay.

They had waited, foolishly. And men armed with clubs and scythes and spears had come and herded them into the village. In the center of the market square there had been a pit. A pit Chakotay had come to know all too well.

Now, as he stood still openmouthed, awaiting the foul-tasting rainwater, he wished with all his heart that he had fled with Tom. Even his second-year Academy training would have set the arm and kept it clean. In a world where five minutes with the Doctor cured broken bones, lacerations, even disease, Chakotay was now vividly reminded of how fragile the human body could be. It had its wonders, too, its miracles of healing, but only so much could be done in a filthy, muddy pit. He did not say so to Tom, and did not want to admit it to himself, but he was growing fearful for his companion's life.

When the rain stopped, there was nearly a third of a meter of mud in the pit. Nonetheless, Chakotay guided Tom down with him and drew their injured bodies close. Warmth, muddy and smelly as it was, was warmth, and right now their chilled bodies needed it.

Impossibly, they fell asleep. Chakotay woke to bright sun streaming in, its light unbroken by the patterning of the grate. Blinking, he stared upward. Someone's head was silhouetted against the blue sky.

"Your Ordeal is over," said Soliss. "For the Crafters' sakes, come out and let me treat you."

CHAPTER
5

As Harry Kim took Khala on a tour of the ship, he couldn't stop thinking about her. Specifically, about her DNA.

How could Khala look so ordinary? She was perfectly humanoid, almost exactly formed like a human save for that beautiful blue that tinted to various degrees hair, skin, and eyes. And yet, she was almost a mirror image of "humanoid" as they understood it. She was one of the most . . . *alien* aliens they had ever met. He couldn't reconcile what he knew about her with the woman he saw, her face animated and curious, her voice soft and pleasant.

And she was smart, too. Her questions indicated a thorough familiarity with all of the physics upon which Federation technology was based. At one point, when he was explaining to her how the bioneural gel packs worked, she exclaimed, "How quaint!" before clapping a hand to her mouth and apologizing.

"Harry, I'm so sorry. I seem to be offending you with every word I say."

"Not at all," he said, and meant it. "We've encountered many different species, both during our time here in the Delta Quadrant and back home. Some are more advanced than we are, some less. But we learn something valuable from every encounter."

"You are very kind," she said. "And I'm grateful for it."

"Tell me more about your people, your planet." He wasn't making polite chitchat. He really wanted to know. He was fascinated by her . . . by her strange cellular structure, of course. Harry wanted to know everything.

"We've met many different races, too," said Khala as they walked down a corridor. "We do a great deal of trade today with off-worlders. 'We' meaning the Alilann, of course."

"Tell me about the Alilann and the Culilann. Are they another species on your planet?"

Her pert little nose wrinkled. "They might just as well be. They're more 'alien' to me than you are. Completely incomprehensible. But no, sadly, they're just a different caste."

"You have a caste system?" The thought disturbed Harry. He'd been raised to think that anyone could do anything he or she set mind and heart to. Even the distinction humans had once drawn between male and female capabilities, which had embarrassingly persisted into recent history, had at last been put to rest. He couldn't imagine living in a caste system, where you were born to a certain role no matter what your innermost longings might be. He was careful not to let his distress show in his voice.

"Oh, yes," she said. "It evolved hundreds of years ago and it's worked very well for both our people. They keep to themselves and their ways, and we do likewise. We are the Alilann. In the old, archaic speech, it means 'seekers of things unmade.' The others are the Culilann, which means 'seekers of things of the world.' "

"That doesn't sound like it would give rise to conflict," said Harry.

"Millennia ago, we were all like the Culilann," said Khala. "We were a primitive people, living in buildings made of wood and stone, eating food we grew, killing animals for their flesh and hides. This was so long ago, there aren't even records, save for paintings on stones. We didn't even have a written language. The stone pictures tell us that another race came from, we realize now, another planet. They preyed upon us and devastated what little there was of civilization. Worse than that, they brought some kind of disease with them. We were nearly wiped out. Only those who fled from the Strangers, as we call them, survived."

"What happened then?" asked Harry, engrossed.

"The survivors were of two minds. Some thought they had displeased their gods, the Crafters, in some way and that to atone they needed to devote themselves totally toward an agrarian life. Others were angry, and wanted to be able to defend themselves should this ever happen again. The two drifted apart. My people, the Alilann, devoted themselves to civilizing our people. We created defenses, weapons, cures for diseases, the ability to create our own food without being dependent upon anyone or anything." She spoke with a great deal of pride. "We developed into the highly technological race we are now."

"And the Culilann?" asked Harry.

"They haven't changed in centuries," she sniffed. "Worshipping their Crafters, digging in the dirt for meager food, living in hovels that leak when it rains. They don't design, they make. With their *hands*. They paint and sculpt and shape clay and fashion something they call 'instruments' that they make noises with. Wasteful activities. If we'd all gone that route, we'd have been exterminated the next time another race decided we were worth troubling with. The Culilann owe their very existence to the Alilann!"

Despite her anger, Harry had to acknowledge that Khala had a point. True, it was one thing to grow tomatoes in your backyard as a pleasant and tasty diversion to supplement your food supply. It was another thing to stubbornly depend on the fickleness of the seasons for your continued existence. Any type of doctor in that society would probably rely on chants and herbs to heal his patients. He'd never swap the Doctor for that. What was in the water? The air? How could you tell without instruments? How could you make sure everything was safe?

But her scorn for the arts and spirituality of the

Culilann disturbed Harry. He'd woken and slept to the haunting music of his mother's various instruments and her singing. He'd mastered dozens of instruments in his childhood. He loved reading good books and tending flowers simply for their scent and loveliness. Art of every sort was in Harry's blood, and it pained him to realize that this lovely woman walking beside him not only did not share his love for art, she scorned it and anyone who valued it.

"Do the Alilann have no art at all? Nothing to adorn their walls, or tables?" he asked, hoping he didn't sound as small and sad as he felt.

"Of course we do," she said, laughing at him. "We have designers. They program images and colors on the computer, and every family has at least one or two."

Harry brightened a little. Even that was something. He briefly recalled a sunny afternoon when he was a toddler. The sun streamed into his room as he messed happily with wet, sloppy, vibrant dollops of color on white paper. Khala had never done that.

He decided to change the subject, though he was still curious about her customs. "I'm surprised you're so friendly to us, actually, since your race has a deep history of being abused by alien races."

"That was a long time ago," Khala replied, smiling sincerely at him. "We think hatred or fear based simply on race, rather than how that race interacts with us, is foolish."

"Boy, I agree with you there," said Harry, almost too heartily. He was so pleased that they'd found some common ground.

"Thanks to our technology, we have extensive communications systems, weapons to defend ourselves if necessary, and interceptors to prevent any aliens we've missed in the conventional manner from falling into the hands of the Culilann."

"What do the Culilann do?" Harry sobered at once.

"They have almost a cultural memory of the Strangers who made war on us and infected us," said Khala. "Without instruments to ascertain if a race poses a threat, then *every* strange person they encounter has to be viewed as a threat. They have something they call the Ordeal. It's positively barbaric."

Khala shuddered, then continued. "They put them in a pit in the center of the village square, dug especially for that singular purpose. A wooden grate keeps them trapped. They are doused with water in a so-called 'ritual bath,' then the Culilann do nothing for these poor interlopers other than pray for them for a certain amount of time. If they survive the Ordeal, they are considered harmless."

Harry couldn't believe it. For the first time, he shared Khala's dislike of the Culilann.

"And it doesn't even work!" exclaimed Khala, as if this were the final straw. "Simply because someone is strong enough to endure a physical ordeal doesn't mean they aren't carriers of a disease that might be harmless to them but fatal to us. That's why we have interceptors, Harry. To find and rescue aliens before they are subjected to the Ordeal."

They stepped into the turbolift. "Engineering," said Kim. There was a slight whirring sound as the turbolift moved smoothly into action.

"I wouldn't want to be stranded in a Culilann village," said Kim honestly. It was the one thing he could find to wholeheartedly agree with Khala about.

The light from the sphere glinted on the metal of Seven's facial implants, turning the silver hue to shiny purple. It was kind of pretty.

"You look good in purple," said Torres.

Seven did not react. Torres guessed she was uncertain as to how to reply, and smothered a grin. One of these days, Seven was going to catch on to something known as "teasing."

In the meantime, their new way of looking at That Damned Ball was starting to yield results, although they had not, as Torres had sarcastically predicted, gotten everything wrapped up by lunchtime. Immediately after they had finished watching the tricorder recording, Torres had adjusted the sensors to scan on the very narrow band that had enabled Telek to locate the Shepherds in the first place. That seemed like such a long, long time ago. Had it really been only a few days? Torres shook her head. Her concentration was being affected by the dark matter the Romulan ships had spewed into their systems. They had to get it out soon.

The scan had yielded immediate results. They were now able to control, to some extent, the amount of power in the orb. At one point, Torres thought she had come perilously close to actually shattering the "unbreakable" sphere. The purple light had grown in intensity and the timbre of the humming sound had soared upward several octaves. She'd shut things down immediately and they'd all stared at each other, damp with sudden dewings of panicky sweat.

They had realized they would have to create another container, similar to but far larger than the sphere. And that container, too, must be unbreakable. But how to get the dark matter in it in the first place?

It was Seven who finally put them on the right track.

"The Bussard collector," she had said.

Telek's brow had furrowed in confusion. "I am not familiar—"

Of course. Smart as he was, he'd only been here for a few days, and he'd been hard at work on the dark-matter problem.

"The Bussard collector is a set of powerful electromagnetic coils located at the front of the warp engine nacelles," Torres explained. "We've used it before to gather up emergency fuel. When the ship is traveling at high speed, the coils generate an electromagnetic field that collects stray atoms of interstellar hydrogen. We can reconfigure the coils, direct them toward the spots where the dark matter is collected, beam it into the Shepherd orb, and from there into . . . into whatever we come up with to contain the stuff."

Telek had frowned. "We cannot dematerialize dark matter. I explained this to you before."

"So, how else do you propose getting the dark matter into the orb?" Torres challenged. "We can't just pluck it like grapes on a stem, you know."

Telek did not answer immediately. Finally, he said, "Can the transporter be adjusted to resonate on the same frequency as the Shepherd technology?"

It was Torres's turn to hesitate. "I think so," she said. "We can try, anyway. It wouldn't be dangerous. Either the stuff will dematerialize or it won't."

It was a relief, almost a joy, to finally have part of the puzzle to work on. They notified the captain of their progress, and Janeway gave her blessing. They then sprang into activity, enlisting everyone in engineering for assistance.

It was into this bustling hive of activity that Harry Kim brought Khala.

"So, this is the warp core," Torres heard Khala saying. She glanced up from her console and nodded a cursory greeting. She expected Harry to give their unusual guest a quick tour and then get out of the way. He must realize how busy they were here. When he didn't, she stepped up to them and forced a smile.

"Khala, I'd love to give you a tour myself, but we're really very, very busy down here. Nonessential personnel should . . ." She faltered, realizing she couldn't think of a way to put it politely. "Should consider themselves nonessential," she finished lamely.

To her surprise, Kim and Khala exchanged grins. "I think you'll find Khala more essential than you imagine. Her people are more technologically advanced than we are, and she's a physicist on her homeworld. I've already acquainted her with the whole dark-matter problem, and she's offered to help."

Torres looked at Khala with new respect. "At this point, I'll take whatever help I can get." Quickly, she brought Khala up to speed. The pretty blue woman followed everything, nodding now and then and occasionally asking for clarification. When Torres was finished, Khala stepped up to the floating sphere.

"The dark matter, as I understand it from what Harry has told me, does not exist in any single universe in its natural state."

"That is correct," affirmed Telek.

"And when it is fully pulled into a single universe," Khala continued, "it is then mutated and rendered harmful. Therefore, in order for the dark matter to be rendered again harmless, it must be removed from a single universe. The logical conclusion is—"

"That Damned Ball is a complete universe unto itself—or else a universe that's all the universes," blurted Torres. "But . . . how? How can that *be,* and how the hell are we supposed to make one ourselves?"

"We will," declared Telek. "We must. Tialin said we could. The orb is the key to understanding everything we need to know in order to complete the quest she charged us with."

"Tialin appears to have a very high opinion of us," said Seven. "I hope it is justified."

Something was nagging at the back of B'Elanna Torres's mind. Something she'd either studied at the Academy or heard of since then. She liked things she could understand, get her hands on, make work at her command. Esoteric theories about alternate universes, the mirror universe, bubble universes, shadow universes—

Bubble. Sphere. Orb.

That Damned Ball.

It was the key to understanding how the Shepherd technology worked—

"Oh my God," said Torres. "I think I've got it. This ball, the orb in which Tialin appeared, your apparatus, Telek, they're all little universes unto themselves!"

"Like my wormholes!" said Telek, catching B'Elanna's excitement.

"A bubble," continued Torres. She turned slowly and regarded the pulsing warp core with renewed interest. "A warp bubble universe. It's been created before."

"That is correct," said Seven. "Stardate 44161.2. Ensign Wesley Crusher and Chief Engineer Geordi La Forge created a static warp shell universe based on Kosinski's theories and equations. Crusher's mother, Chief Medical Officer Beverly Crusher, was trapped by the warp shell and found herself in a universe of her own making." At Torres's expression, she explained, "Captain Picard was assimilated by the Borg. I have done a great deal of research about the history of the *Enterprise*."

She gazed levelly at Torres. "The incident proves that while such a shell can be created, it cannot be made stable. It required the assistance of an alien called the Traveler, whose species has the ability to exploit the interchangeability of time, space, and thought, to rescue Dr. Crusher. I do not think placing massive quantities of dark matter inside such a bubble universe is a wise idea."

"But somehow the Shepherds have done it," protested Torres. "They must have the same ability as the Travelers. They gave us the key to understanding their technology!" Angrily she snatched the glowing, hovering orb from midair and waved it under Seven's nose. "Tialin *said* we could do it."

"We can," said Khala quietly. "We have conducted such experiments ourselves at great length. We, too, were never able to make it quite stable, but with the Shepherd technology as given to us with the orb, I think we could do it."

As one, they all fell silent. Torres knew precisely what was going through their minds because she was certain it was the same as what was going through hers: all the myriad things that could go wrong, any one of which could spell death.

Oh, the theories *sounded* solid enough. They'd sound better over a cup of *raktajino* and a pile of sandwiches at the end of a long shift, when they would remain precisely that—theories, not something they were going to try to put into action.

Torres felt certain that the Bussard collector could be adjusted to perform as needed. Telek's theory about the specific frequency could easily be tested in action with no danger. It was only if everything worked according to plan that there would be risks.

What if they couldn't stabilize the warp shell after all? Or what if it seemed stable, then collapsed? How would the warp drive work with a mini-universe in its heart that was filled to the brim with dark matter?

The only thing worse than failing was not to try.

"Let's do it," she said.

CHAPTER
6

JEKRI GAZED AT HER REFLECTION IN THE MIRROR AND decided she did not like what she saw.

She was in full dress regalia, and the uniform hung limply on her slim frame. She had lost weight these past few weeks. She was not surprised. Her mind had been consumed with thoughts first of recovering Telek R'Mor and capturing *Voyager,* then with suspicions about the arrogant Shepherd ambassador. A further strain had been her need to hide the latter thoughts. She did not put anything past Lhiau. Murder was entirely possible if he thought Jekri Kaleh posed any kind of real threat.

Her face was pale, the cheeks hollow, the eyes encircled by darkness. She scowled and reached for a seldom-used stash of cosmetics. She did not like to wear them; such vanities were for softer females, not for the chairman of the Tal Shiar. But it was important that she draw as little attention as possible, and her present haggard appearance would not pass unnoticed. After applying a base coloring to give some warmth to her sallow skin and some quick swipes of green to tint her cheeks, she scowled even further. She looked dreadful. *This* would attract more notice than her unadorned, tired-looking face. Jekri washed off the cosmetics and scrubbed her face clean. Better.

She ran a quick comb through her short, silky black hair, and she was ready.

Why a banquet? There was little enough to celebrate. Earlier, the Empress had demanded hourly reports from Jekri's team of scientists and spies. Jekri recalled the image of the weeping Empress and realized that even though she, Jekri, had not made the hourly reports from time to time, there was no contact from the royal household about the lapses.

The Empress hadn't noticed.

Jekri frowned at her image in the mirror. She had not gotten where she was without trusting her hunches, and now the prickling at the back of her neck was telling her that something either was very wrong or was about to go very wrong.

And whatever it was, it concerned the Empress.

The banquet was held at the palace. By the time Jekri arrived, proudly unescorted, most of the other guests were already present. She took a small goblet of blue Romulan ale from a server's tray. Sipping the potent beverage carefully—Jekri never allowed herself to become intoxicated at formal gatherings—she surveyed the room with a silver-eyed gaze that missed nothing.

The magnificent entry hall was festooned with colors and decorations, all as fierce and proud and commanding as the Romulans themselves. No pretty ribbons or flowers here. No, there were shields and armor from ancient times and bold swathes of rich-hued fabrics. Music came from somewhere—live performers, a luxury only the rich could afford. It was soft and lovely, designed to soothe the guests and encourage them to eat, drink, and talk freely.

Jekri would do none of these.

She looked for any survivors of the disastrous attack on *Voyager*. If there were any, they would be hailed as heroes, despite the debacle. They would be honored, simply because there had once been so many and now were so few. Jekri saw none, and felt a twinge of grief. Either none had survived or they were too ill to attend. Whichever it was, it was sobering.

There were a few of the senators, chatting pleasantly, drinks and small appetizers in hand. Their faces were bland and fixed in polite expressions. Jekri wondered why they bothered. Everyone here tonight, even the lowest-ranking among them, was a key political figure in some way. Everyone had an agenda. No one was the bland, polite guest he or she so desperately wished to appear. At least she didn't bother with the pretense. She was the Little Dagger, and everyone knew daggers were sharp.

Verrak had not been invited. He was not of sufficiently high rank. For that, Jekri was sorry. She had come to rely upon him over the years they had spent working together, and trusted him as she trusted few people.

The Praetor caught her eye. He paused in midsentence and his face grew flat. He nodded coolly.

A chill raced up her spine. Keeping her gaze locked with his, Jekri returned the nod of acknowledgment. She recalled the words of the Praetor: *I think you may have overlooked something, and I think you need to get back into the Empress's good graces very, very quickly. And I think, Little Dagger, that you need to watch your back.* She returned to scanning the room.

"You're slipping, Little Dagger," came the nasal, high-pitched drawl of the Praetor. Startled, Jekri whirled. He had managed to come up behind her completely unnoticed.

"Either that or your stealth skills are improving," she said, keeping her voice calm. "Have you tried the ale yet, Praetor? It's quite a superior vintage."

"The Empress's cellars are stocked with nothing less than superior vintages, and always have been," replied the Praetor quietly. His dark eyes flitted about the room. He did not look directly at Jekri. "It's not like you to waste time in idle conversation."

"It's not like me to be at formal functions at all," said Jekri. "Yet the Empress seemed adamant that I attend, even though I have her work to be about."

"It's not at her command you're here," said the Praetor. He nodded toward a small circle of people who had entered the room in a cluster. At their center was the tall, handsome alien calling himself a

Shepherd. Lhiau laughed and beamed and in general tried to conduct himself like a jolly ambassador. It made Jekri's stomach churn.

"It's at his."

Jekri's heart lurched. Her face revealed nothing, of course; she would not let it. Why did Lhiau particularly desire her here tonight? What nasty little surprise was in store for her?

"Watch yourself tonight, Little Dagger." With that ominous declaration, the Praetor stepped forward and blended into the crowd.

At that moment, Lhiau slowly turned his head and looked directly at Jekri. He smiled, and that smile could not have been more unsettling if he had had a mouthful of pointed teeth.

Still don't like me, eh, Little Dagger? Pity. We're both on the same side, you know.

The voice was inside her head, every bit as mocking as if Lhiau had uttered the words aloud. Jekri did not look away. She thought of the smooth taste of Romulan ale, of Verrak's strong body, of the little mind-puzzles that sometimes absorbed her whole attention. She thought of everything but how much she disliked and distrusted Lhiau.

His beautiful features were marred by a slight frown for a moment. *Got you*, Jekri thought before she could censor it.

For a moment only, Little Dagger. For a moment only.

The sweet jangling sound of the ritual summoning bell broke the link. It was time to head into the feast hall for dinner. Jekri summoned her strength, did her utmost to mask her thoughts, and entered with the others.

The Romulans were proud of their heritage. Most important buildings were models of efficiency, contemporary sites with up-to-the-minute technology and comforts. Only the palace remained as a monument to the past, though even its trappings of bygone eras were essentially a facade. There were torches, hearth fires, and candles, but the room was climate controlled, and there were alternative forms of lighting available. The plates and the food items they held would be sent back to the replicators after the meal. The private rooms, Jekri knew, were as contemporary as her own offices.

But the candle's flame burned like any other, the ale was real, and the chairs and tables at which the guests seated themselves were genuine antiques.

Jekri did not care if she sat on a chair built yesterday or one on which an emperor of centuries ago had placed his royal posterior. She had not scrabbled in the dirt of the poorest province on the planet for riches and the trappings of decadence. She had done it for power, and now that power was in jeopardy.

There were name cards, another outdated and annoying tradition, and it took the assembled guests some time to find their seats. Jekri headed for the head table, her usual place. It was with a sickening feeling that she saw, next to the Empress's center seat, not her own name but that of Lhiau. Her heart began to race as she scanned the table.

She was not even *at* the high table tonight.

For the briefest of moments, panic seized her. She

lifted her head proudly and strode toward the nearest table, searching casually for her name.

Jekri Kaleh, Chairman of the Tal Shiar, was toward the end of the third table out of five.

It could be worse, said the voice in her head. *You could be at the last table. Or not invited at all.*

Perhaps I should not have come, Jekri thought coolly. *I do have my business to be about, after all.*

You came when called, like the fvai *you are,* Lhiau sent savagely. Jekri winced in pain. *And you'll bark when I tell you to.*

Jekri Kaleh was no stranger to hatred, but never before—not when her body was at the mercy of thugs in the street, not when groveling before a brutal master, not when she had been forced to murder a friend to save the reputation she had so carefully crafted—had she known the white-hot, sweeping flame of hatred that swept through every cell at this moment.

She had to stop this. She had to stop Lhiau from crawling around inside her brain as if it were his right.

Jekri pulled back the chair and sat. On either side were lowly civil servants and their mates. She realized that her being at this table was causing a mild sensation, and she tried to appear calm, as if she normally sat with these—these—instead of at the left hand of the Empress.

With as much casualness as she could muster, Jekri looked toward the head table. At the center, of course, was the Empress, resplendent in a low-cut, clinging gown of diaphanous purple material. The jewels that adorned throat, ears, and hair gleamed of gold and lavender.

On her right was the Praetor, who looked perfectly at ease. Sitting in Jekri's accustomed place, of course, was the hated Lhiau. Jekri's lip curled in disgust as she watched him fawning over the Empress, contriving to touch her hand or shoulder, brushing a phantom lock of hair out of her eyes. What was even worse was how the Empress visibly blossomed under Lhiau's attentiveness. Her expression grew softer, the painted green lips curling up into girlish laughter. Her eyes never seemed to leave his.

The full horror of it smote Jekri. Lhiau was seducing the Empress! Not with charm or gallantry, not if she knew him, and Jekri knew she did. He was worming his way inside the Empress's normally keen mind. The Praetor had already told Jekri that it was Lhiau who had arranged for Jekri to attend. There could be only one reason for that.

Lhiau leaned close to the Empress and whispered something into her delicately pointed ear. She laughed, and as she pulled back from Lhiau her gaze fell upon Jekri.

At once, the full lips thinned. Her eyes narrowed.

Jekri tasted full, real fear for the first time in a long time. She hoped desperately that she would walk away from this evening's activities still chairman of the Tal Shiar. Then she amended that hope.

Jekri Kaleh hoped she would walk away from this evening's activities at all.

The Proconsul, seated to the Praetor's left, rose. He lifted a goblet of blue ale. "A toast!" he cried.

There was the sound of dozens of chair legs

scraping along the stone floor as those assembled rose and lifted their glasses.

"To the glorious Romulan Empire!"

Shouts of hearty agreement filled the room as everyone quaffed their ale. Jekri sipped only a little; there would be more toasts and nine courses through which to nurse this glass.

"To the Empress! The brightest star in the Empire!" the Proconsul continued. Usually these toasts were the right of the Praetor, but everyone knew how the Praetor detested public speaking and avoided it when he could.

They drank the health of the Empress, the Praetor, the Proconsul, the Senate. Everyone was about to sit down when Lhiau rose, surprising them.

"One final toast," he said in a rich voice, lifting his goblet high. "To the absolute and total conquest of the quadrant!" He turned to the Empress. "Lady, tell them the good news."

The Empress beamed as she rose, her gown rustling softly. "My dear, good friend Lhiau is correct," she said, her voice carrying in the suddenly silent hall. "While we are still very much interested in retrieving the traitor Telek R'Mor and the Federation starship in the Delta Quadrant, Lhiau and I have decided that it is time to intensify the plan. We do not need to wait for *Voyager* to begin amassing a fleet the likes of which the Federation has never seen."

Jekri's eyes were glued, not to her Empress, but to Lhiau. That he felt her attention was obvious by the slight smirk that quirked his lips, but he remained focused on the Empress. The profound depth of his hypocrisy amazed Jekri. Had the man absolutely no sense of honor?

There is no honor required when dealing with kllhe, came Lhiau's hot response.

He knew precisely what to say to anger her. Of course, he would. He was inside her mind, curse him. She licked her lips and did not respond.

"Lhiau has agreed to give us whatever we require to get our fleet ready for invasion," the Empress continued. "Whereas before we had thirteen, soon our numbers shall be nearly uncountable. And when we do succeed in retrieving *Voyager* and Telek R'Mor, why then, the Federation vessel shall be our flagship. We shall discover what it was that so tragically brought down our thirteen lost warbirds. We shall see that such incidents do not recur. And when we sweep down upon an unsuspecting Federation, victory must needs be ours!"

Jekri couldn't believe what she was hearing. Surely, logic dictated that they first determine what went wrong with the thirteen cloaked ships before placing the devices aboard an invasion fleet. Lhiau had said something about the wormholes doing the damage; Jekri had her doubts. Lhiau knew much more than he was telling. Jekri needed to find out what that was.

And what was his plan? Hitherto, he had given out the dark-matter cloaks only grudgingly, and even then only to the ships that had been sent out with the express purpose of finding *Voyager.* Now he was handing them out with abandon and seemed to have forgotten his driving quest of recovering the way-ward scientist and the Federation ship.

"Little Dagger," came the Empress's smooth voice, chilling Jekri to the bone with its icy timbre. "Come forward."

Jekri rose and strode boldly to the high table, executing a quick bow. "Your Excellency?"

"What are you doing here?" The Empress's anger was not even veiled anymore.

"I received an invitation, Your Excellency, and did not think to insult you by not attending," Jekri replied.

"You received no invitation," said the Empress. Jekri thought of the crisp cream envelope, a throwback to an earlier time, which had been hand delivered, of the name card on the table where she had just been sitting. For a long moment she stared at her liege. She had known the Empress for years, had watched her grow from a precocious young girl into this stunningly lovely, brilliant woman.

Before her sat a stranger, and the knowledge was alarming.

Jekri bowed again, lower this time. "My apologies," she said, her voice controlled. "My assistant must have been mistaken. With your permission, then, I shall take my leave and return to where I may do the Empire the most good."

"In your subcommander's bed?" snapped the Empress. Snickers went around the hall and Jekri turned bright green.

Slowly she smiled, her silver eyes hard and angry. "Nay, Your Excellency. He comes to mine when I call him."

The snickers turned to laughter and there were smatterings of approving applause.

I have to get out of here, Jekri thought, feeling something akin to panic even as she turned to face the crowd and accept their applause.

Yes, came Lhiau's thoughts. *You certainly do.*

"You may leave us," snapped the Empress.

A third time Jekri bowed, and, head held high, she strode at just the right pace out of the hall. When she got out into the foyer and the huge, ornate doors closed behind her, she slumped against the base of a statue, trying to slow her racing heart.

"Is the honored chairman well?" It was a servant. His inquiry was polite enough.

"It was a trifle warm inside the feast hall," Jekri answered. "But I am well enough." She nodded and left. She could feel Lhiau's contempt snapping at her heels like a pack of wild *fvaiin.*

He had brought her here to humiliate her. He had turned the Empress against her, and wanted her to see it. Jekri's position, perhaps even her very life, hung on a slender thread, and Lhiau pulled that thread.

No one in the Romulan Empire was safe from him.

She did not return to her ship, but to her offices in the capital. Jekri chafed at the time, only a few seconds in reality, that it took for her to pass the various security measures. She had her eyes, fingerprints, DNA examined and was finally let into her own office.

Like everything about Jekri Kaleh, the office of the chairman of the Tal Shiar was in scrupulous order. No digging through awkward piles for her.

When she needed something, she was able to place her fingers on it within moments.

She found the file she needed and called it up on the computer. It was a routine report handed in by one of her field spies. A few weeks ago, swamped by the urgent need to find Telek and the starship, she had scanned the thin file and dismissed it. There were always dissidents. One had to judge who was dangerous and who was not.

These she had filed in the latter category, but now she hungrily perused the file as if it contained her salvation.

Because, she realized, it probably did.

INTERLUDE

THE ENTITY'S FIRST ENCOUNTER WITH THE STRANGE, frightening matter of which the Presence had warned it went smoothly. The matter was drifting alone in space, a cluster of something that was once right and natural and had been made terribly wrong. The Entity felt sorry for it. It had had no choice. Gently, the Entity engulfed the wrong things into itself, rendering them harmless.

They did not fight; they had no sentience. But the Entity wondered if that was entirely correct. After all, the Entity was no corporeal thing, trapped in a body. And it had sentience. It thought comfort, and peace, and was content in its task.

Again and again, it sought out what the Presence

had called corrupted dark matter and pulled the tiny bits into its mammoth, limitless self. It was an easy task, a joyful task, and one that had at its end a great and wondrous purpose.

A few times the Entity found the wrong things in the hearts of stars; sometimes in the bones of planets. It moved with a timeless grace to gather up the pieces, extracting them from other matter with an ease that it did not know it possessed.

It moved at a speed that was unknowable to places unseen, harvesting the wrong things like a child plucking flowers.

It knew a faint ripple of discontent. A child plucking flowers? How did it know these things? Dimly, something that might have been memory stirred, and the Entity was confused.

Its confusion increased when it came to a planet populated by sentient beings.

Because it recognized them.

CHAPTER

7

TELEK AND SEVEN STOOD TOGETHER IN ASTROMETRICS.
Torres and Khala stayed behind in engineering, ready
to shut everything down the minute any danger was
perceived. They had consulted with the senior staff
for suggestions and received the captain's approval
for this first trial run. Yet they all hesitated. Telek was
familiar with the grip of fear and the paralysis it often
caused, and he was the first to shake it off.

"R'Mor to Torres. We are prepared. Is everything
in order in engineering?"

The briefest of hesitations, then, "We're ready. Go
ahead."

The simulations they had conducted on the
holodeck had varied wildly. One scenario had shown

everything proceeding perfectly until the final step. Another had shown almost the exact opposite— things went wrong at the outset. A third granted them partial success. Each time, save for that single, nearly perfect one at the very beginning, something different had gone wrong. They were starting to run out of time; the amount of dark matter was growing at an exponential rate. Thus far, it hadn't caused any major damage to flesh or equipment, but Janeway had given the command: *Do it.*

"Then let us begin," said Telek.

Even the self-assured Seven of Nine seemed hesitant, her metal-clad fingers hovering over the controls before she began to tap in the proper sequence with a deft touch. Telek monitored her progress from another console.

"Section fourteen, mark six," said Seven. "There is a large cluster of dark matter."

"An excellent test subject," said Telek, his voice perhaps a touch too flat in his attempt to keep any trace of nervousness out of it.

"I will attempt to lock on to it," came Khala's voice. They had rerouted the transporter through engineering, the better to be able to watch everything at once and perform emergency shutdown procedures if needed.

This, as far as Telek was concerned, was the trickiest part. He had conducted dozens of experiments with dark matter in the laboratory. Never had they been able to lock on to it with a transporter, let alone dematerialize it. The stuff wasn't ordinary, baryonic matter, as he had told them repeatedly. How could you—

"I've got it locked," said Khala, her voice higher and filled with pleasure.

Telek and Seven exchanged pleased glances. Even the former Borg was tense and excited, Telek saw.

"Remarkable. Well done, Khala," he said heartily. Torres's theory about utilizing that unique frequency shown to them by the Shepherds was, thus far, working beautifully. He moved to stand beside Seven. She had adjusted the computer sensors to visually depict the cluster of dark matter. There it was on her screen, a pulsing blip of yellow color in the lower right-hand corner. Telek swallowed hard.

"Attempting dematerialization," said Khala.

Before their eyes, the yellow blip faded and disappeared. Telek let out a huge breath he didn't realize he had been holding. The dark matter was now dematerialized, ready to be rematerialized inside a safe container.

He and Seven sprinted to engineering, not caring that they ran to the turbolift. Seconds later, they entered engineering to see Khala and Torres struggling not to grin. They weren't out of the woods yet, and they all knew it. But they had passed the first barrier to success.

All activity in engineering save that directly involved with transporting the dark matter had ceased. Torres's team stood quietly, watching raptly.

"Okay, Khala," said Torres. Her gaze was fastened on the hovering sphere. "Transport into the sphere."

Khala touched the controls. The steady, pleasant hum the sphere had hitherto emitted turned into a screeching groan that assaulted the ears. The light grew bright, brighter, searing the retina, and Telek was forced to close his eyes even though he wanted to watch, wanted to see what would happen next.

This was surely the end. They had miscalculated, and this close to the dark matter, they'd all be dead within minutes. It would shatter the sphere, invade their bodies, phase them in and out of existence, and—

The hum ebbed. The light dimmed.

The little ball's light was now bright red, not purple, and they could see millions of tiny specks floating safely inside it.

"The second step has been successfully accomplished," declared Seven, as if they couldn't all see it for themselves.

"I'm constructing the warp shell," said Torres, her fingers flying. "Khala, transport on my signal . . . now!"

Again the terrible sound filled engineering, and again the bright light, blood red this time, nearly blinded them. When the sound and light both faded, the ball was once more its serene hue of purple.

They stared at the green warp core. It appeared to be no different to the naked eye, but Torres was looking at her console. They waited. Seventeen point four seconds was the longest the warp core had lasted, even in the best simulation they'd run on the holodeck. Telek was aware that he was trembling, but felt no shame at the thought.

"Eighteen seconds," said Khala. "Twenty. Twenty-five. Thirty." A pause. "One minute."

One by one they relaxed. Telek closed his eyes briefly.

"It could still destabilize at any second," Seven warned them darkly.

"But it's lasted longer than any simulation. We could all die at any second. That's what life is all about, Seven," said Torres, her voice cheerful despite the dolorous words she uttered. "I say we get on with the next step."

"We've beaten all the simulations," said Telek. "I suppose it is due to the fact that the holodeck can only operate or extrapolate from something it knows. And none of us knows the full extent of Shepherd technology."

"That little sphere is amazing," Torres admitted, gazing with a new respect at the small, hovering ball. Telek suspected she wasn't going to be calling it That Damned Ball again any time soon. She tapped her combadge. "Engineering to bridge. We've got a warp-core universe full of dark matter, and we're all still in one piece."

"*Qapla'*, B'Elanna," came Janeway's warm, pleased voice.

They did it again. And again, and again, each time increasing the amount of dark matter they beamed in from the transporter to the sphere to the warp-core shell. There was no sign of strain.

The next step was to attempt to dematerialize the dark matter from inside something—a cup, the ship, a body. But by this time, simple biological need was beginning to take precedence over the thrill of success. They broke for lunch and went to the mess hall. When the door hissed open, a huge cry of "Congratulations!" greeted them.

"We thought you could use a break," said Janeway, smiling as they entered. The place was festooned with banners and balloons. Tables had been decorated, and on every one there was some kind of confection with the words "Dark matter" written on a card beside it: Dark matter cake, dark matter cookies, dark matter pudding.

"All made with the utmost care to suit the palates of *Voyager*'s daring engineering team," said Neelix with pride as he hastened up to them, shaking their hands vigorously. To Khala he said very gently, "There was, of course, no time to bake anything, so I had to replicate everything. Please enjoy without worrying."

She blushed blue. "Neelix, how thoughtful of you. Thank you."

Janeway paused before Telek, turning her piercing blue gaze on him. "As a scientist, you must be finding all this very exciting." She smiled. "I know that, as a scientist, *I'm* excited by what we're doing. As a captain, of course, I'm even more excited that we've survived it all thus far."

Telek smiled a little himself. He arched an eyebrow and said, "Why, Captain, did you have any doubt?"

She searched his expression for a moment, then the smile broadened. She reached to squeeze his arm.

The food, replicated or not, was delicious and filling. At Torres's insistence, Telek had his first sip of *raktajino*. He found it powerful but delicious, and he had a second cup. Some items called "tomato soup" and "cheese sandwiches" were also unusually tasty. Perhaps it was merely that he knew—he *knew*—they had cheated death today, and everything about being alive, including food, had a keener edge of pleasure about it.

He was well into an enormous slice of something rich that Neelix called Dark Matter Double Chocolate Chip Fudge Cream Cake when Janeway, who was sitting beside him sipping a cup of black coffee, got the news from the bridge.

"Tuvok to Janeway."

"Janeway here. What's going on, Tuvok?"

"Sensors indicate a large fleet of ships approaching in our direction. They are heavily armed and shielded. And they are also riddled with dark matter."

Telek set down his fork. Suddenly the deliciously sweet treats and the two cups of potent *raktajino* sat like rocks in his stomach. He wished he had not attacked the food so eagerly. If there was a fleet of heavily armed ships permeated with dark matter on an intercept course, their intentions could only be hostile.

Perhaps death had decided it did not like to be cheated after all.

"Yellow Alert," said Janeway, sliding into her command chair. "Shields up. Battle stations." *Though I hope it doesn't come to that,* she thought. *Wiping out those thirteen Romulan warbirds, watching them explode to bits because of the dark matter they carried—that was hard enough.* "On screen."

It was every bit as bad as she had feared. Several ships were headed right for them. They were large, cumbersome-looking things. If Janeway had to guess, she surmised they were heavier with weapons than with engines. These things were built for battle, not speed. If the need arose, *Voyager* could probably outrun them.

But that's not what we're here to do, she thought with a sudden surge of fierce passion. *We're here to help them, to free them from the dark matter if they're infected with it.*

"Harry," she ordered, "scan for dark matter."

"Scanning," Kim replied. "They're crammed full of the stuff, Captain. People and vessels."

Janeway thought a deep, profound curse. "B'Elanna, what's the status on getting the dark matter out of objects rather than just from space?"

"Not good, Captain. We didn't have a chance to run any tests."

"Is Dr. R'Mor with you?" Janeway inquired.

"I am here, Captain."

"Of all of us, you're the most familiar with the dark matter. What's your opinion?"

A long pause. The ships were moving ever closer. "It has shown no signs of distress or instability thus far," he said, and she could hear the caution in his voice. "One would hope that this would continue, but there is, of course, no guarantee."

Janeway had been all for her hardworking team in engineering to take a well-deserved break at the time. Now, she wished they'd at least tried to extract dark matter from a coffee cup, or a plant, or anything at all. But they hadn't. One always made the right decisions in hindsight, didn't one?

"Mr. Kim says the approaching ships are filled with dark matter," Janeway informed the Romulan. "How would you propose removing it?"

"The separation point would probably occur within the transporter mechanism itself," came a clear female voice. For a moment Janeway couldn't place it, then she thought: Khala. "It could be risky trying to locate the dark matter within the individual molecules at the point of origin, especially when dealing with an unknown, unfamiliar cellular structure. I would recommend total dematerialization and the separation of the dark matter particles at that moment."

"I see," said Janeway, her blue eyes on the approaching vessels of war. From what she understood about the process, she felt Khala was right.

But what did that mean for them? How in the world were they going to conduct a first contact with a hostile species and then ask for the kind of trust that was going to be required? *Hello, you're a totally new species and you're filled with a maddening hatred that's actually not what you're feeling at all. Let us dematerialize you, remove the bad thing and then put you together again. And let us do that to your ship and crew as well.*

Oh, how she wished Chakotay were here. She'd love to hear his take on the situation. But she was now, as she always had been from day one of this strange voyage, the captain, and every decision ultimately rested with her.

"Mr. Kim," she said, her voice betraying none of her growing sense of hopelessness, "do we recognize this species at all?"

"Negative," said Kim.

"Bridge to Seven. Take a look at our new friends. Do you know them?"

"Negative," came Seven's crisp, cool voice. Same word, same distressing information.

"Open a channel," said Janeway, squaring her shoulders. "This is Captain Kathryn Janeway of the Federation *Starship Voyager*. We are on a peaceful mission in your sector of space and would like to open communications. Particularly, we wish to warn you about a danger to your crew and vessel of which you are more than likely unaware. Please respond. Let us open a dialogue."

Nothing. The ships just kept coming closer.

And then they powered their weapons.

CHAPTER

8

THE DESERT SUN WAS BRIGHT AND HOT, AND BURNED him. The sand was bright and hot, and burned him. Chakotay was bright and hot, and burned inside and outside, and even his eyeballs seemed to sizzle in their sockets as he tried to look around.

He wore no uniform. In fact, he wore nothing. The hot sun beating down on his exposed flesh would, he somehow knew, crisp it in moments. His first thought was of Tom, and that pale, Anglo-Saxon white skin that went with blond hair and blue eyes, and what the bright, hot, burning sun would do to it.

"Don't worry about Tommy," said the voice. Q's voice. The voice of a Trickster par excellence. "You should be worried about yourself."

"Coyote," said Chakotay. He recalled being aboard *Voyager* when the dark matter had not yet been purged. He had utilized the *akoonah* and gone deep within his subconscious in a quest for guidance. His usual animal guide had not appeared. Instead, he had faced off with Coyote, an incarnation—perhaps the ultimate incarnation, he mused—of the classic Trickster deity. It had spoken with the voice of the omnipotent alien Q, and it was using that same taunting voice now.

"The one and only," said Coyote, trotting over a sand dune, rising on his hind legs, and executing a bow. "Or should I say, one of many?"

"The last thing I remember was trying to climb a ladder out of the pit." It had been like exiting a kiva, he had thought at the time. Except kivas weren't places of torture. He recalled putting his left foot on a rung, then the right—then nothing at all.

"Out of the frying pan, into the fire," quipped Coyote, citing a proverb that was nearly as old as the stars. He trotted down the dune, miraculously not disturbing a grain of the bright, hot, burning sand.

"What do you mean?" asked Chakotay, a desperate tinge to his voice, even though he knew that getting anything resembling a straight answer out of the infuriating creature was well-nigh impossible.

"Do I say what I mean, or mean what I say?"

"Alice in Wonderland," said Chakotay at once, though it had been decades since he'd read the children's book.

"Welcome to the rabbit hole," said Coyote, and he vanished.

When Chakotay opened his eyes a few seconds later, it was not at all bright, or hot, or burning, though his body still was fighting a fever. He lay on his back in a small thatched hut. He was covered with a blanket of some soft, woven material. The pile of—hay? ferns?—beneath him was soft and comfortable. It emitted a cool, soothing scent as he stirred. Over his head herbs hung drying from every inch of the roof. He tried to move his head and look around, but the gesture brought sudden pain and he hissed.

"You mustn't move, Chakotay," said a soft female voice. A hand moved into his vision, a hand holding a cloth that dripped cool water onto his face. Chakotay closed his eyes and enjoyed the unbearably sweet sensation of a moist cloth wiping his fevered face. A drop trickled to his lips. Automatically, he licked it and savored the taste of cool water and herbs.

"You stood for hours with your face turned up to the sky," the feminine voice continued. "Your neck is still stiff and sore."

"Where am I?" he asked, his voice a rasp. "Who are you? Is Tom—"

"Tom is recovering, as are you," came the answer. He couldn't stand it; he turned his head and beheld she who tended him. The pain he suffered with the action was worth it. She was lovely, a vision come to life. Her full lips curled in a smile.

"I see your curiosity outweighs the pain," she said. "I am Yurula. I am mate to Soliss. He is presently out gathering more herbs for a soup for you. He predicted you would awaken soon."

"I thank you for your care of us," he said. The pain in his head was agonizing. It was hot, so hot.

"Rest again," Yurula urged him. He watched, his vision blurring slightly, as her blue-tinged hands dipped into the wooden bowl of water, wrung out the cloth, then again placed its welcome coolness on his brow.

He obeyed her gentle command, and when he woke again, the light in the cottage was different: softer, dimmer. He could still smell the sweet scent of the bedding, but there was another smell that he couldn't quite place. He felt cool, and much stronger. His body was damp.

"Your fever finally broke," said Soliss, moving into the chair beside Chakotay's bed. "Would that I could say the same for your companion. Are you in any pain?"

Chakotay considered. His hand went to his abdomen, touched the bandages there. "It still hurts a little," he said, reluctant to complain after he had so clearly been well taken care of, but realizing the importance of telling his doctor—his healer, at any rate—everything. "It's sharp and localized, though."

"Good. I can't take away all the pain all at once, though it is my understanding that some of the doctors among the Alilann can."

Chakotay thought of the Doctor, and said nothing.

"But at least we stopped the rotting before it went any further. Just a nice, clean wound now. You're strong and healthy, you should be fine. Are you hungry?"

The word seemed to trigger something inside Chakotay. It was as if it had flipped a switch. He had been so sick that his body was concentrating on healing itself, not on acquiring nourishment, but once Soliss had suggested the idea of eating, it seemed like the finest thought in the world.

"Starving," he confessed.

Soliss smiled. "I thought you might be."

As he rose and went to the cook fire in the center of the single-room cottage, Chakotay realized what the other smell was. It was food, though of what type he was not sure, and his hunger flared again. He propped himself up on an elbow, realizing that he was naked beneath the blankets. He hoped that Soliss had been the one to tend him and that the radiant Yurula had been called in only after the wounds had been cleaned. Chakotay chuckled to himself. If he was able to worry about who had seen him nude, then he was definitely feeling better.

His mirth faded as he gazed across the room at the occupant of the other pallet. Tom still looked bad. He moved restlessly in his sleep, and his face was flushed. Now and then he muttered something.

"You said Tom wasn't healing as well as I," said Chakotay.

Soliss was ladling soup from a hanging pot into a bowl. "No, he isn't. I've done everything I can, but his injuries were far worse than yours." Suddenly Soliss frowned. "That cursed Ordeal. I hate it, I hate it."

The crude wooden door opened and Yurula entered. "Shame on you, Soliss!" she cried. "I could hear you from several steps away. Would you have us banished?"

"Apologies, beloved," said Soliss, though he didn't

look particularly apologetic. "It is only—You know that if I had been permitted to attend to them once they were brought here, they would be well on their way to health now, both of them. The Ordeal—"

"Is part of what makes us who we are, as surely as turning our faces up to the sky and eating the fruit of the good soil," said Yurula. Her face softened. "I love you for your heart, Soliss. But perhaps it is just a little too soft."

She turned and smiled at Chakotay. "You look much better than the last time I tended you. How do you feel?"

"As much improved as I look, I imagine," Chakotay replied. "Ready to eat some of that delicious-smelling soup." She went to him, checking his pulse and feeling his forehead. At one point, to better gauge the temperature, she pressed her cheek to his forehead. Chakotay breathed in the scent of herbs and her own sweet, musky fragrance. Yes, he was definitely feeling better.

A thought occurred to him. He looked around for his clothing and saw no trace of it, nor of their instruments.

"We can understand each other," he said suddenly. "My communicator—"

"There is no need for such things," said Yurula, a touch forcefully. "My mate has spoken with you over the last few days and it is easy enough to learn your language."

She was right. She had been speaking Federation Standard the whole time. He'd been too out of it to notice. "That's incredible," he said. "Your people must have a gift for languages."

"The Crafters gave it to us," said Yulura. "It is so that we do not need to resort to the artificial contrivances of the Alilann. They would be able to learn as swiftly as we, as we are the same species. But they do not have the desire. They prefer everything to be immediate. They do not wish to take the time to learn a skill."

Chakotay thought back to what life must have been like without the universal translator, what an accomplishment simply learning another language used to be.

"We are both—" He had started to say "humanoid," but realized how Earth-centric the term was. "We are both bipedal and shaped much the same. Our mouths and throat structure are probably very similar. Can you learn the language of races more unlike yourself?"

"They take a little longer, but we can do it if we need to," said Soliss. He rose, carrying a bowl of steaming soup. Chakotay's mouth watered. Yurula helped prop him up with the pillows while Soliss handed him the bowl.

Yurula made as if to take the bowl and feed him, but he smiled and shook his head. "I can do it myself, thank you."

She nodded her blue-haired head in acknowledgment and rose gracefully. Chakotay guessed her age at about thirty or forty in human years. Yurula was not possessed of the youthful freshness of the girl who had found him and Tom, but she had a quiet beauty all her own.

Chakotay spooned up some soup, sipped cautiously, then began to eat with gusto. It was delicious. Plenty of fresh vegetables, rich broth, bits of meat of some sort. Normally he'd use his tricorder to make certain the food wasn't toxic to his system, but right now there was no choice: eat, or die. And if he died, at least his taste buds would have been placated.

He handed the empty bowl back to Yurula, who smiled at his appetite. "Would you like some more?"

"Yes, please. It's delicious."

"Before you have a second bowl," said Soliss, "please put these on. If my guess is right, we may have need of your bed soon."

"More injured?" Suddenly Chakotay wasn't hungry. He reached for the soft robe-like garment Soliss handed him, spun by Culilann hands, and slipped it over his head.

"No," said Soliss, chuckling. "A blessed event. It is almost Winnif's time. I would not turn a sick man out of bed, Chakotay, but I'd want to make sure a woman giving birth has a comfortable place. If you will pardon me, I am going to see how she fares."

Chakotay found himself smiling. *Life does go on,* he thought. His mind went back to the last time he had seen his shipmates. Were they all right? Janeway had accepted the Shepherd's so-called quest to locate others and help them rid themselves of the deadly dark matter. Had they been successful? Were they able to utilize the alien technology, put it to work for a good cause? And what had they learned about Khala, the poor, misplaced Alilann? Had she told them about these craftsmen and farmers, healers and weavers?

Were they looking for him?

Would they find him?

He ate a second bowl of the delicious and no doubt nourishing soup. He had to get his strength up if he and Tom were to leave. Chakotay had not endured the Ordeal in a pleasant frame of mind, but he had known kindness at the hands of Yurula and Soliss, and he was not going to make a sweeping condemnation of these people. They had their own ways, and Chakotay respected that. Yet it was becoming increasingly clear to him that the only way he and Tom could hope to contact *Voyager* was to contact the Alilann first and make use of their technology.

He finished the soup, worked the soft robe about his frame, and swung his legs to the floor. The soles of his feet tingled, as if they had not touched earth in far too long. When he rose, he was unsteady on his feet, and if it had not been for Yurula's swift movements he would have fallen. She slipped beneath his arm and held him up.

"Come sit by the fire," she said, "while we change the bedclothes."

He wobbled a little as he walked, but made it to the fire. Yurula eased him down and began to gather the soiled clothes. She stirred the herbs on which Chakotay had been lying, bruising them and sending a burst of fresh scent into the air, then placed clean cloths on the bed.

Chakotay turned his attention to Tom, who slept on. Chakotay thought that sleep was probably the best thing for the injured conn officer. There was a ceramic carafe and cup beside Tom's makeshift bed, and Chakotay guessed they got a little bit of water into him from time to time.

His own wounds had been superficial—a sprain, simple skin lacerations, nothing more. Yet even his injuries had become infected and gangrenous. Tom's had been much worse. A broken arm, with the bone poking through the skin—bad news even under the best conditions. Here, it could be a deadly threat.

Hang on, Tom, he thought fiercely.

The door opened and Soliss entered, guiding an extremely pregnant young woman. It had to be the aforementioned Winnif. Chakotay mentally congratulated Soliss on his observation; he'd been right on target about today being Winnif's time.

She beamed from ear to ear, showing no signs of the pain that human women endured. Chakotay remembered what Seska had once told him, back in the days when they were lovers. He'd expressed some concerns about pregnancy. She had told him that if she did get pregnant and chose to carry the child to term, the birth would be easy on her as she was a Bajoran.

Of course, Chakotay mused bitterly, she hadn't been a Bajoran, but a Cardassian spy. And she had gotten pregnant, but not by him, though she had tried.

He shook his head, trying to dispel the bitter memories, and focused on the simple happiness that the young woman emanated. Yurula eased her onto the bed, smiling along with her, and Soliss placed a beautifully carved and painted screen in front of the bed so that the birth might occur in private.

An astonishingly short time passed, and then Chakotay heard the lusty wail of a newborn crying for air.

Life. It went on.

The pleasure ebbed as he saw Yurula, with tears on a face that was nonetheless staunchly resolute, rush out the door with the crying baby. He couldn't hear what Soliss murmured to the young woman, but her cry of anguish shattered the air.

"No! *No,* not my baby, I have prayed, I have done nothing wrong, no, no—"

"I am so sorry, but the Crafters have called for your child. It is an honor, Winnif, an honor."

But Winnif sobbed and sobbed, and Chakotay knew that the new mother felt that whatever was happening to her baby, regardless of Soliss's calm, gentle words, did not feel like an honor to her.

"Let me take you home," said Soliss. "You should be with your family now." Physically, Winnif seemed well enough, aside from her tear-streaked, blank face. Clearly, recovery from birth was instantaneous in this race. The door closed shut, and Chakotay was left alone.

The Crafters, he surmised, were the gods of these people. Perhaps the baby was born with a mark that indicated he was to be raised by whoever served the Culilann as shamans, or priests. Such a separation would be hard on a mother, but surely such a child would be well looked after and loved.

After a time, Soliss returned. He looked as though he had aged a decade. Wearily, he sat down by the fire. For a long time he did not speak. Chakotay respected his silence. Finally Soliss rose and went to Paris. He checked his vital signs and eased the ensign up into a sitting position. As Chakotay had suspected, Soliss got a little water down Paris's throat, then laid him down.

"You have seen only the harshness of our people," he said, not looking at Chakotay. "We must seem like the worst of primitive barbarians to you. You have undergone the Ordeal, and now must witness the Surrender. Would that you could see our brighter, more life-affirming celebrations. Well, you will, once you are healed."

"I don't understand," said Chakotay. "You said the baby had been claimed by the Crafters. Is he or she to be raised in a holy house of some sort?"

Now Soliss did look up, and grief warred with anger on his face. "The holiest house of all," he said. "The house of Nature itself. The child was born with a clubfoot. We are not permitted to keep such children. Yurula has taken it to the sacred mountain and left it there for the Crafters to take. They always do. At least," he added, "something always does. In my darker moments, I fear that it is not the Crafters, but their predatory children, the beasts of the woods. There are not many of them, but what there are, particularly the *islaak*, are fearsome. And prey is scarce these days."

Chakotay stared at the bleak expression. He felt the blood draining from his face. Now he recalled that every person he had seen here had been whole and straight. No blindness, no missing limbs, no twisted spines, nothing that one might expect from what was essentially a primitive culture. There was no one who was even remotely homely among their number. Now he knew the reason for that.

The Culilann killed their imperfect children, and sweetened the horror with a sugary dusting of faith.

CHAPTER
9

JEKRI HAD SAID NOTHING, NOT EVEN TO VERRAK. BETter that he not know. That way, he could not be forced to tell. She, of all people, knew that if the Tal Shiar wanted to know something, it had the means to do so. She had merely told him that she was pursuing another lead and that she would be periodically out of contact over the next few days.

She had forgotten how beautiful the outskirts of the city of Tal K'shir were. Certainly, an effort had been made in the city to have the occasional garden or grassy area, but that was a pale imitation of the vast expanse of green, growing things that stretched to the horizon here, away from the city. She had seldom ventured beyond her offices and her vessel.

Sometimes she felt like a spider, wrapped securely in her web, thousands of tiny strands reaching from her to the outside. Jekri's intelligence officers were all individually selected for loyalty, intellect, and evidence that they knew how to think on their feet. She respected all of them and trusted most of them.

But she was on her own now, lingering over an ale in a tavern while the soft, muted light cast everything into comfortable shadow. In the corner, a single flute player piped a soft tune. In the heart of the city, it was cheaper to use computerized music; live performers were prohibitively expensive. But out here, the songs that came from a player's fingers cost very little. Outfitting the entire tavern with a computer system was not an option.

Despite the urgency of her mission, Jekri felt the tension melt off her shoulders like wax. Had it really been that long since she had put aside her uniform and spent some time simply sitting in a tavern?

The ale was strong. Surely that was it. Jekri took another sip, a small one, and her silver gaze flitted around the tavern for the hundredth time.

This tavern was the hotbed, her source had assured her. Jekri had rolled her eyes at the term. A handful of Romulans whispering in a tavern was hardly a "hotbed" of anything. She had dismissed the report, filing it away. Now, she was glad of the thoroughness of that intelligence gatherer. It could save her life.

Two Romulans, a male and a female, entered together. They tried to move casually, as if they were no more than a couple patronizing a tavern for a drink before dinner, or perhaps before something more intimate. And they probably would have fooled anyone else, but Jekri had almost a sixth sense about deception. She had practiced it enough to recognize it in another's manner.

The laughter was too loud. The movements too free. And the way they kept looking about, although it was painfully obvious that they were trying not to be noticed, practically shouted that they were here not for an innocent ale, but for something much more risky.

She continued to watch them as they took a seat in the darkest corner of the room. The pale green illumination globe on their table was the only light, but it was enough for the sharp-eyed Jekri.

Jekri couldn't hear their conversation over the droning sound of the flute and the chatter of the other patrons, but she didn't need to. She had a clear line of vision; that would suffice. Reading lips was a skill she'd mastered almost before she had reached puberty.

"He told me he won't be able to attend the meeting tonight," said the woman.

"Is he being watched?" asked the man, his body language revealing his anxiety.

"He's not sure and he doesn't want to risk it."

Jekri smiled to herself. No one was watching these people, except of course for her.

"Perhaps we should move the meeting place," the woman continued, her uncertainty plain on her face even as she pretended to peruse the list of alcoholic beverages the establishment provided.

"I think you may be worried over nothing," said the man, reaching out to cover her hand with his own. "We're small, yet. There's nothing for the Tal Shiar to fear."

You're half right. The Tal Shiar couldn't care less about you, thought Jekri. *But the chairman of the Tal Shiar . . .*

"The children are starting to ask questions, according to Mairih," said the woman.

"Then let her bring them," said the man. "I still have the toys I played with as a child, and I know you do too. We have no children to pass them on to. Let us give them to Tonna and Dral."

A server stepped forward, blocking Jekri's view. She waited patiently as he took their order and moved away.

Eagerly the two returned to their illicit conversation. Jekri wondered if they were more interested in doing something forbidden than in the theories and culture they were allegedly devoted to reviving.

She was disappointed that they spoke aloud, even though it made it fool's work to eavesdrop on their conversation. She had hoped—well, she was unwise to hope. Perhaps the skills she sought to learn from these people could not be taught. Perhaps all they did was gather clandestinely, read old books, and dream of a future that could not possibly happen. Perhaps they did not truly study the disciplines. She had seen such things in so-called "enemies of the state" before—not a genuine yearning for something different, only a desire to be daring and rebellious, to do something illicit for the sake of doing so, not for any real cause or belief. She hoped she was wrong about this particular group.

The couple now began to chat about aimless things, and though she continued to watch their lips move, Jekri learned nothing new. They ordered soup and a salad of greens. It looked good. Jekri had the same thing, and was surprised at how delicious real food, freshly prepared, tasted to her. She had been living solely on replicated fare for months, perhaps years. Food had become little more than a source of nutrition, and it was certainly not an occasion for pleasure.

She paced her meal with theirs, finishing as they did. They did not rush through their meal, but did not seem to be enjoying it overmuch. Now and then the female would glance around. Jekri willed herself to melt into the background, and the woman's eyes slid right over her. The chairman of the Tal Shiar could command the attention of the entire Senate with a word or two, or she could be utterly inconspicuous if she so chose. That was an old, old skill, one that had saved her life in dark alleyways and taverns far more run-down than this one.

The specter of her past had long arms, and Jekri willed the memories away. She valued the skills the past had taught her, but she had no wish to linger there overlong. She lived in the present, and in the present, the couple she was stalking had paid and were leaving.

Jekri did likewise, scattering a few coins on the table and heading out the door before her targets. She huddled in the darkness of an alley, her back pressed against chill stone, as they exited and strode purposefully down the street.

In her early days with the Tal Shiar, she had been given many assignments like this. She smiled a little, recalling those days. She had been a hissing, spitting cat of a girl, full of rage and a desire to prove herself. No one had expected her to be as disciplined as she was, as skilled at silence, stalking, and striking. But she was then, and was still. She followed the utterly unsuspecting couple through the twists and turns of the dark streets, through the fields that boasted swaying harvests of grains and fruits, and down a dirt road. Ahead was a small stone house. The lights were on.

The couple did not complete their journey alone. In small groups of one or two, others joined them. They sometimes embraced the newcomers, hoisting a small child affectionately. By the time the group had arrived at the stone house, their number had swollen to eleven, if one counted the children.

Jekri hesitated. Normally, if she wanted to infiltrate this group, she would have marked the meeting place and turned and left in silence. She would concentrate on one or two of them, befriend them, win their trust with the occasional "slip" of the tongue that showed she was sympathetic to their cause. Gradually, they would decide she could keep their pathetic little secret and invite her to one of their meetings.

But that would take time, and judging by her treatment at the banquet, time was short and growing shorter. Jekri did not have the luxury of a perfect infiltration. Bolder measures were needed; a gamble had to be taken.

She weighed the options. Few in the common populace had access to energy weapons of any sort. And considering the values this particular group claimed to espouse, weapons and aggression would be the last things Jekri would find inside the stone walls of that building.

She took a deep breath and squared her shoulders in the earth-hued, makeshift robes she'd managed to find. She felt for her own weapon, hidden in the long, rectangular sleeves. A quick shake would bring it right into her palm if she needed to use it.

"Fortune favors the brave" was an Earther's saying that had found its way into the Romulan tongue, and Jekri knew it was right.

Boldly, she strode toward the door. She did not knock. She gripped the knob, twisted it, and opened the door.

She heard gasps. It would have amused her, had her mission not been so dire. There they sat, two dozen or so men, women, and children. They occupied every chair and every inch of the floor. Children played with small triangular toys inscribed with strange markings; Jekri could guess at their meaning. The eldest one present was in the center of the room, a book spread across her knees. That ancient tome alone would have condemned her without another word being said. As one, they all stared at Jekri in horror, their eyes wide, their mouths open with shock.

"My name is Jekri Kaleh," she stated. "I am the chairman of the Tal Shiar. I am armed and prepared to use my weapon if necessary. This is not a raid. I demand that you teach me everything you know about Vulcan mental disciplines, or I shall kill you all."

There was no immediate response. Jekri grew irritated. "You," she said to the woman holding the book. "You are Dammik R'Kel, aren't you? A few of the rest of you are her children and grandchildren. We have all your names on file. At any moment, we could seize you, your homes, and everything you own. I have no wish to do this, but I do require your knowledge."

Still silence. Jekri locked eyes with the matriarch, Dammik R'Kel. *Can you read thoughts, old woman? Has studying Vulcan disciplines taught you how to do that?*

No immediate response, as with Lhiau. In fact, the woman's face didn't change. Disappointment knifed through Jekri. What would she do now?

"Why do you wish to learn this, child?" said Dammik in a deep, mellifluous voice. "I know why the rest have come, but from what I know of the Tal Shiar, they would call what we are doing here treason."

"Mother!" snapped the young man Jekri had followed to his parent's house. "There's no need to tell her anything." He lifted his chin. "You followed us. I remember you from the tavern. You'll learn nothing here. We will die first."

"Don't tempt me," said Jekri.

"Karel!" rebuked Dammik gently. "That is not the Vulcan way. We will share our information with all seekers. Surely Surak would be pleased that one so well-placed in the government is interested in learning about Vulcan culture." Her dark eyes returned to Jekri, and though the old woman had given no hint that she possessed the skill of telepathy, Jekri felt as though that gaze bored into her soul. She shook the thought away.

"She does not wish to learn Vulcan culture!" continued Karel. "She wants to trick us, to trap us!"

Before Jekri spoke, a young woman, barely out of puberty, replied, "That would not be logical, Uncle. She already knows enough to convict us or she would not have been able to identify Grandmother. You are thinking with your emotions, not your mind." The girl turned to regard Jekri with her grandmother's piercing gaze. "Although," she said, "It is possible that the honored chairman wishes to learn Vulcan skills in order to exploit them, not use them in accordance with IDIC."

"Infinite diversity in infinite combinations, I know," replied Jekri tersely. "I will be honest with you." She lowered her weapon, knowing that the gesture would be interpreted as a trusting one. "I am no idealist. I am interested in my personal security, and any mental skills I can learn from you would further that very important goal. Look at it this way. You could betray me as easily as I could betray you."

Some of them bought the lie, but the oddly mature girl only smiled slightly. "Hardly," the girl replied. "You can arrest us. We have no means to do the same without risking our own safety."

"Fair enough." Jekri liked this girl. "You seem like someone I can talk to—" She lifted an eyebrow in question.

"Tarya," the girl replied. "And the final decision lies with my grandmother."

"Well, Dammik? Teach the chairman, or go to prison?"

"Logic dictates that I have no choice but to tell you what you wish to learn," Dammik answered.

"I'm beginning to like logic," said Jekri.

Once their leader had spoken, the others fell in line, though it was clear that many of them mistrusted her. They tried to tell her about the children's toys, which contained the syllabic nucleus of the Vulcan language, but Jekri wasn't interested in learning to speak the language of emotionless pacifists. They then started to read from the ancient tome in Dammik's lap, but Jekri interrupted.

"I did not come for a history lesson," she snapped. "I wish to learn about the mental disciplines. Controlling emotions, thoughts, the nerve pinch, mindmelding."

"You are not Vulcan," replied Tarya pertly. "How do you expect to be able to mind-meld when your biology isn't the same?"

"We both descended from the same common ancestor," Jekri retorted. "In evolutionary terms, the schism was not so long ago. Romulan and Vulcan brains should be identical."

"Similar, but not identical," said Dammik. "The Vulcans have spent centuries actively training their brains to work in certain ways. We have neglected these areas and they have fallen into disuse, like a limb will if it is not exercised."

"This is not what I came here to be told, old woman," said Jekri menacingly.

"Lies will not endear you to our cause," Dammik said placidly.

"I do not *care* about your cause. Come, surely there must be something!" Jekri burst out.

"We can begin with this—controlling your outbursts," said Dammik. "I imagine such a skill would be extremely useful to the chairman of the Tal Shiar."

"My temper is under my control."

"Perhaps, when you deem it to be useful. Perhaps when you are negotiating with an ambassador, or the Praetor, or the Empress, you can control what you say and how you behave." Dammik leaned forward. "But you must learn to control it at all times. You must not insult a child whose plaything has made you trip, or a servant who has prepared the wrong food, or an old woman who is doing her best to help you because she senses you are in danger."

Jekri stared. Slowly, Dammik smiled. "I am not a telepath," she said softly, "but it does not require one to read your mind. Why else would you come to us with such an offer of clemency?"

Jekri chose not to protest. "Then help me," she said.

They began by doing a group meditation. Jekri was jumpy and anxious to plunge right into more active exercises and had trouble following Dammik's instructions to calm her mind and slow her breathing. Her mind was as active as a *nei'rrh*, flitting from branch to branch, idea to idea. Reluctantly, she admitted that Dammik was right about her. She did not have the level of control she wanted; she merely had suppression. That was something quite different.

"Keep bringing your mind back to the rhythm of your breath." Dammik's voice floated to Jekri, who had not, at that moment, been concentrating on the rhythm of her breath but rather on the Empress, Lhiau, and her chances of success. She did not want to concentrate on her breath, she wanted to—

No. This was the key. In her heart of hearts she knew it. Control began here, at this moment, with this single thought, this single breath. There. She did it once, she could do it again. She inhaled, held the breath for an instant, exhaled through her nostrils. It was not so hard.

"Now," said Dammik, "go deeper. Feel the breath in your blood, in every cell. Loosen your jaw." Jekri's was clenched, and obediently she parted her upper and lower jaw, keeping her lips closed. Better.

Go within. Inside was the control she sought. At the very core of Jekri Kaleh's identity, safe from fear, from worry, from desire. She found her inner center, and approached it with not a little awe. All her will, her determination, her grit—it was not these things that were her strength. It was this quiet pool in the cavern of her soul. She could almost see it as a cavern, cool and dark and moist. In her mind's eye, she knelt at the obsidian pool that was her heart, cupped the liquid, and drank deep of her inmost self.

This would be her shield. This would be her victory.

This would break Lhiau's hold on the Romulan people.

The thought was joy incarnate.

INTERLUDE

THE RECOGNITION WAS VAGUE, BUT IT WAS THERE. THE Entity knew this place, though it could not determine how. Names came into its consciousness: Baneans. Numiri.

There had been people here once. Feathers? Something about feathers, and a knowledge of the mind. Great science was here, and great rage. Now, there was only a desolated planet. Any life that was here was primitive: grasses, microbes, bacteria. Great sorrow welled inside the Entity, for the presence of the wrong things was great here, and it knew it was their darkness that had turned a cool war into devastation.

It swept through the star system, mourning. It em-

braced the barren planet and obtained knowledge, it did not know how, that pain and torture had been part of the depletion of the planet. The Baneans had used their knowledge of the brain as a weapon, forgetting higher, more enlightened goals; the Numiri, not needing much urging, had retaliated with a violence that had forever rendered this planet unable to support life.

Were they extinct, the Baneans and the Numiri? Had they slain one another down to the last individual? The Entity did not know. But one thing was certain: the dark matter had done this. The Entity gathered the wrong things up, containing them, purging the poor wounded planet from their continuing malice, and, grieving the tragedy, moved on.

CHAPTER

10

THE BRIDGE WAS ILLUMINATED WITH BLOODRED LIGHT. On the screen were eight heavily armed vessels of a race as yet completely unknown to the crew of *Voyager*. Their weapons were powered up.

"Brace for impact," said Janeway in a flat tone of voice, betraying nothing of the fear that was always present in moments like this.

"They are firing," said Tuvok, his voice as expressionless as his captain's.

Janeway curled her fingers around the arms of her chair, bracing as she had told her crew to do. But the expected attack did not come. Instead she watched as, to her shock and bafflement, the lead enemy vessel proceeded to destroy one of its own ships.

"The shields on the seven remaining vessels are down," said Tuvok.

"What the—" began Harry, who shut up immediately.

"I'm with you, Harry," said Janeway. "Send this message: We do not wish to fight. There is no need for a suicide mission here. You have nothing we need. We only want to help." A sudden blinding insight flashed across her mind. "We are coming closer to offer aid."

"Captain," said Tuvok, "if we approach the fleet, we are likely to incur damage from the exploding vessels if they continue to destroy themselves."

"I'm counting on them to realize that too, Tuvok." She threw him a quick glance. "Trust me on this. Good old-fashioned human intuition."

"Captain, we're being hailed," said Kim.

"On screen."

An angular, mottled face filled the screen. Despite the deep, sunken eyes, beaklike mouth, and lack of a nose, the face was humanoid enough that Janeway could recognize the signs of deep grief and despair etched on his features.

"Captain Janeway, please leave this area of space. We've done enough. We have no desire to harm innocent species any further. Let us destroy ourselves in peace."

"I've no intention of letting you destroy yourselves," said Janeway, rising and walking down to the screen. She made no attempt to hide her emotions now. "What is it you think you have done that warrants such extreme measures?"

The being looked down, then up again at Janeway.

"Several months ago, we killed the populace of an entire solar system. The Katian system. All gone, all dead."

"Harry," said Janeway, "I think we passed through that system not too long ago. We've certainly been there since they have, and I don't recall it being devastated. Find it and report the minute you can confirm or deny that statement." She turned again to the screen. *Keep him talking,* she thought.

"Were you at war with the inhabitants of the Katian system?"

"We are not a warlike race," said the alien. "We fight only as a last resort. War is not orderly, and we prize order above all things. These vessels are defensive only, built merely for protection against aggressors. They usually remain in our home system."

"Then how is it you managed to wipe out an entire solar system?" Janeway pressed.

The alien did not answer. He looked confused. "I—I don't remember. But they're dead, all dead!"

"Captain," said Kim, "You were right. We passed through the Katian system less than two weeks ago. At that time, the six planets of the Katian system were inhabited by billions of sentient life forms. There was no residual evidence of any battles fought there, no trace of pandemics, nothing. Those people were fine when we saw them, and I bet they're fine now."

Janeway nodded, her eyes on the alien. "You are filled with despair, aren't you? Hopelessness, a sense of futility. You see wrongs that you have done and you feel that the only way to . . . to atone is to kill yourselves. Am I right?"

He blinked solemn eyes that had no whites. In a voice harsh with self-loathing, the alien replied, "You know us well, Captain. Is it so obvious that we are—" He choked for a moment, then continued in a thick voice, "We are abominations, that even an alien can see our obscenity?"

"No," said Janeway softly, her own voice thick with compassionate pain. "What I see is that your crew and your ships are filled with something called dark matter, and it's affecting your judgment. The inhabitants of the Katian system exhibit no damage. Your recollection of destroying them all is a false memory. It never happened."

"No!" He clung to his delusion like a drowning man to a floating log. "No, they're dead."

"They're all right," Janeway repeated. "We can send you the data."

"False! We have records, we—"

"Your memories and computer systems cannot be trusted. Think about it—you can't even remember what you did to decimate an entire system! We have dealt with this crisis ourselves. Our ship was damaged, and so were our minds and bodies. Our scanners indicate that you are carrying a great deal of this matter. We know how—" She paused, then chose the word deliberately, "—how evil this matter is, how it corrupts mind and body. Please, trust us. Let us help you."

For a moment, hope brightened the strange face. Then he lowered his head. "We are beyond help. We can only hope to rid the galaxy of our corruption. I intend to give the order to destroy every vessel in the fleet, and then I will begin to attack my homeworld.

Only when we are utterly destroyed as a race can the universe be free of our . . . our . . ." He stopped, obviously unable to find the word to express just how horrible a blight his people were.

Janeway had heard what she needed to know. This being was the one to give the orders. She would begin with him.

"Their shields are still down. Tuvok, drop ours on my command. Kim, lock on to him and beam him directly to sickbay, then terminate communication. Now."

Tuvok dropped the shields. Kim immediately executed his captain's order, and Janeway watched as the alien disappeared from his own bridge. His crew jumped up in horror, then the screen was filled with stars and ships. At once, Kim's station began to sound with a frantic beeping noise.

"Tuvok, you have the bridge. Mr. Kim, don't answer their hails until I tell you to. I'm betting that they're not hostile. They want to kill themselves, not us. At least, I hope so." She headed for the turbolift. It seemed to take forever to get to sickbay, but at last she reached it.

"Captain, what are you doing? Please, I must be allowed to complete this!" The alien was seated on a bed while the Doctor ran a tricorder over him. He looked confused and upset, but didn't appear to be fighting.

Janeway ignored him. "Any resistance?"

"None," the Doctor replied. "Would that all my normal patients were so amenable to being told what to do."

"What is your name?" she asked.

"Ulaahn," he said, "but—"

"Janeway to engineering."

"Torres here."

"Torres, lock on to the alien Ulaahn in sickbay. Dematerialize him and keep his pattern in the transporter buffer."

Ulaahn opened his mouth to protest. But for the second time in the space of a few minutes, the baffled alien was dissolved into molecules without his consent.

"Khala, you said that you could separate the dark matter from the true matter at this point?"

"Yes," came Khala's excited voice.

"We're working on it right now," said Khala, her blue fingers flying over the controls. "I'm instructing the computer to locate and isolate all the dark-matter particles. It seems to be working."

Torres hovered over her. At another station, Telek and Seven watched the process, their heads bent over the console and almost touching. They all knew that if the computer missed a single particle, or if a single normal molecule was mistakenly culled, their visitor would be dead sooner or later.

"Got it," said Khala. "Torres, would you check?"

The other three examined her work. "It appears to be complete and accurate," said Seven.

"All right, Captain," said Torres. "We're as ready as we'll ever be. Khala, reassemble Ulaahn in sickbay." Under her breath, she said to her team, "Cross your fingers."

Seven frowned. "What purpose would it serve?"

"More than you might imagine," Torres shot back, and waited to hear from her captain.

Janeway held her breath as the familiar whine of the transporter filled sickbay. She wondered if it was taking longer than usual, if the image that was manifesting before her eyes would have some terrible flaw.

And then there he was, looking stunned and not a little offended. He straightened and strode up to her. "How dare you abduct a Kwaisi captain! This is an insult, an outrage!"

She smiled in relief. Good, simple, healthy anger. Gone was the cowering, despairing figure about to assassinate his own people and himself in the mistaken belief that they deserved such treatment.

"But, Ulaahn," she said mildly, "what does it matter what we do to you? You deserve to die, remember? You were about to annihilate your own species. Shall we beam you back to your vessel and let you continue?"

The black eyes widened. "So I was," he said, softly. "I was about to—Fate forgive me, I *did* destroy one of—Captain, how did you effect this cure? What wondrous thing have you done?"

"No wonder," said Janeway, "just science. But time is crucial here, Captain. You need to speak with your people before it's too late."

"Open a hailing frequency to Ulaahn's vessel," said Janeway as she and the alien strode onto the bridge from the turbolift.

"Captain!" exclaimed the paler alien who was

clearly Ulaahn's second-in-command. "You just disappeared. We didn't know what to think!" His thick lips turned downward. "Though any end would have been fitting, after what we have done."

"Orric!" snapped Ulaahn. "Listen to me. I am commander of this fleet, and I am about to issue a direct order. No one will disobey it."

Orric seemed chagrined. "Of course, as ever, I listen, Captain."

"I have agreed to permit Captain Janeway to transport everyone onto her ship, one by one, and to have full run of our vessels until such time as I deem fit. Is this understood?"

Orric cocked his head. His voice was full of confusion. "Yes, Captain. Understood. Though it will only prolong our eventual and much-desired self-destruction."

"Never mind that," said Ulaahn. In the turbolift, he and Janeway had agreed that trying to convince the other Kwaisi that the dark matter was the real threat was a waste of precious time. Obedience was all that was required now, and from what she was gleaning of Kwaisi culture, obedience would be granted. There would be ample opportunity for discussion once the crew members were all returned to their right frame of mind. "You are trained to obey your captain. Obey him now."

"I shall, Captain."

Ulaahn turned to Janeway. "Prepare to beam my crew aboard, Captain. They are in your capable hands."

* * *

By the time they had transported thirty Kwaisi and completely eliminated all traces of dark matter from their systems, Torres was beginning to feel cautiously optimistic. At one point, during a brief break, she glanced at the hovering ball with something akin to affection. They were all getting used to the awful screeching noise the ball emitted every time they utilized it as a conduit for the dark matter. Seven had adjusted her ocular implant to account for the bright, bloodred light so that she, unlike the others, was not forced to look away and could continue working.

With Janeway's permission, they rotated their own crew with those of the alien vessels. One by one, slowly but steadily, the crews of all the ships were being purged of the deadly dark matter. Everyone in engineering had been transported and reassembled. Torres couldn't speak for everyone, but she knew she felt calmer and more stable now that she knew the dreadful stuff was no longer in her tissues.

So far, everything was performing without a flaw. Khala was monitoring the status of their warp bubble universe and just kept nodding her head every time. All was well there. It pleased Torres to watch the affected Kwaisi enter as hostile, frightened, or otherwise mentally disturbed beings and emerge after the transport slightly stunned and sometimes sheepish, but sane.

Results. Torres liked results.

"Lieutenant Torres," came Seven's cool voice.

Please, no problems, not now that we've finally figured this out. "What is it, Seven?"

"Because of the adjustment to my ocular implant,

I have been able to monitor the sensors during the last several transports. There is something you should all see."

Torres exchanged glances with Telek and Khala. Silently, they all left their posts and went to stand beside Seven's console.

"At the precise moment when the dark matter is transmitted into the sphere," said Seven, "there appears an encircling field of some sort of radiation. It dissipates almost immediately once the dark matter is transferred to the warp-core bubble."

She deftly touched the controls, and an animated graphic appeared. "I shall play back the sensor readings of the last three transports. Observe."

They watched in apprehensive silence as the graphic displayed the process of dematerializing one of the aliens, separating his healthy molecules from those of the dark matter, and placing the dark matter particles into the orb.

Exactly as Seven had described, a perfectly spherical field suddenly appeared around the Shepherd's orb. It lasted only as long as the dark matter was contained within it, and then it quickly dissipated. Twice more, the same thing occurred, except—

"Damn it." Angrily Torres rubbed her eyes and blinked. "I'm hoping I'm just tired and my eyes are playing tricks on me, but I don't think so. Seven, check this for me. Is it just me or is the radiation field around the orb growing larger with each dematerialization?"

Quickly Seven did the calculations, then gazed at Torres with new respect. "You have excellent vision,

Lieutenant. You are correct. The circumference of the radiation field around the orb has increased point zero six percent with each transport." She looked at her colleagues in turn.

"I believe this has been occurring ever since the orb was activated. There is no indication as to the purpose for the manifestation of this field, or whether it is harmful."

Torres turned and stared at the hovering purple sphere. It was their only hope to remove the dark matter from these affected, infected people. And now it was emitting some sort of field that grew more powerful every time they used it. What were they going to do? The orb was all they had.

"That damned ball," Torres said, with feeling.

CHAPTER 11

INTERCEPTOR SHAMRAA EZBAI REMILKANSUUR WAS convinced that the trauma of seeing his sister disappear right in front of his eyes had rendered him temporarily insane. It was the only explanation. Otherwise, he would never have opted to lead a recovery party at all, let alone think such a thing would be "fun."

How could he have forgotten the unpleasantness of the sim runs he had undergone as part of his training? A holosim training exercise was grueling enough, and there was always a shower and clean clothes and fine, replicated food waiting for him at the end of the ordeal.

Now he was out with his team of ten subordinates, sitting in a hot, steamy jungle while hot, steamy rain fell for what seemed an eternity. There had been nothing real before this rain. His life before now had been an illusion, a fantasy, a dream of dryness and temperate, artificial climes. And there would be nothing after this rain. It would continue, inexorably, until it had washed away their clothing from their bodies, their flesh from their bones.

In short, Ezbai was utterly miserable.

Next to his skin, which was soaked beneath several layers of clothing, which also were soaked, his communication device vibrated. On a mission such as this, a sound would give them away. They wore their commdevs on their chests. Ezbai called a halt and rummaged through his clammy garments to retrieve the device.

It was a message from the Order:

Am in receipt of a transmission from the Silent One. Change course to two point eight seven mark eight, to the site the Culilann call the sacred mountain. There is a small cave at the base and you will need to issue a recovery.

Ezbai wanted to groan, to weep, to fling himself on the sodden, stinking soil and pound it with his fists. The course change would add several hours to what was already becoming an almost unendurable mission. Still, he knew what a recovery at those coordinates meant, and there was no way he'd not want to make that kind of recovery.

He kept reading: *The two aliens have been released from their Ordeal. The larger of the two, named Chakotay, is recovering well. The slighter, called Tom Paris, fares ill. We do not think his life is in danger; however, recovery from the Minister's domicile will be more difficult. We will keep you posted as to new developments.*

Then, nastily, the Implementer had written, *Hot enough for you?*

Ezbai resisted the temptation to hurl the commdev into the brush. Instead, he tried to dry it off—futilely—and reattached it to his skin.

His crew were taking advantage of the halt in hiking to drink water and eat some food. "Finish what you've got in your mouths and put the rest away," he told them. "Course change. We're to go to the sacred mountain, two point eight seven mark eight. A recovery will await us there."

A chorus of groans and protests arose, competing with the hum of insects. Someone suggested what the Culilann could do with their sacred mountain, and in his heart, Ezbai agreed.

"Primitives," snarled Ioni, his second-in-command, as she hoisted her pack. "Dirty, stinking, feebleminded primitives."

It crossed Ezbai's mind that at the present moment he was dirty, he probably stank, and he had certainly been feebleminded to volunteer to head this mission, so he said nothing. Grimly, the recovery team reversed course to heading two point eight seven mark eight.

The days had passed uncomfortably since Yurula had taken Winnif's baby to the sacred mountain. The warmth Chakotay had felt toward these people, the admiration for the way they clung to their traditions and their faiths, was now offset by the brutality of some of those traditions.

He was alone in the Minister's hut, helping to prepare the midday meal by chopping some long, sweet-smelling roots, when he heard Tom's voice.

"Hey," said Paris weakly.

Chakotay whirled. "Tom," he said, not bothering to keep the warm rush of pleasure out of his tone. He knelt beside Paris's pallet. "Welcome back."

"Not sure I want to be back," said Paris. "I feel like hell."

"You've pretty much been there for a while," Chakotay agreed. "What do you remember?"

Tom's brow, shiny with the healthy sweat that meant his fever had broken, furrowed. "Not a lot," he confessed. "I remember the cavern, and you jumping through some kind of portal." His pale lips curved into a smile. "There was this girl. She was pretty stuck-up, but boy was she gorgeous." The smile faded. "And rain. I remember rain, and mud. And that's about it."

Briefly, Chakotay filled him in. Tom remembered nothing of Soliss or Yurula. He had slept through the Sacrifice, and when Chakotay told him of it in sad tones, he shocked Chakotay with his response.

"How do you know they're not doing the right thing?"

Chakotay stared. "Tom, they're taking a helpless infant and leaving it on the side of a mountain."

"No, no, I mean how do you know that the Crafters aren't real?"

Chakotay laughed, a harsh, disbelieving bark. "That fever must have hit you pretty bad. I'm usually the one making the case for the divine. You're one of those I'll-believe-it-when-I-see-it types."

"Well, they're certainly not gods, but how do we know that they aren't aliens who appear to be gods to this culture? You said that Soliss said the babies are always taken."

"He thinks they're taken by predators, not the Crafters," said Chakotay.

"But others don't. All I'm saying is, don't jump to conclusions. For all we know, some aliens may be watching the Cu—Cully—"

"Culilann," supplied Chakotay.

"—Culilann and sending someone down from a ship to rescue the kids."

Chakotay regarded him sadly. "That's a nice world you live in, Tom. Maybe you shouldn't rejoin our reality just yet." He rose. "Can you get up? You've been lying down on the job for too long."

Paris flashed him the faintest ghost of his trademark devil-may-care grin and tried to lift himself up. His elbows slid out from under him. Chakotay was there, easing his fellow crew member up, wrapping a blanket around him, and helping him toddle on rubbery legs to the fireplace in the center of the hut.

"Thanks, Mom," said Tom, hugging the blanket around him. "How about some chicken soup?"

"Maybe later if you're a good boy," Chakotay replied. "In the meantime, I'd better keep chopping these vegetables if we're going to have anything to eat for dinner."

The door opened. Yurula entered, carrying a woven basket full of herbs. Chakotay saw something that looked like a purple loaf of bread peeking out over the top of the basket.

"Paris!" she exclaimed, pleased. "Were you able to get to the fire on your own, or did Chakotay help you?"

"I am as yet unable to stumble to the fire on my own," said Tom, sounding more like his old self with every minute, "but I remain confident that someday I will be able to feed myself."

She chuckled.

"I understand that we have you and your mate to thank for our survival," Paris continued. "I'm sorry I haven't been able to express my appreciation sooner."

"You were in no condition to do anything but eat, sleep, and get better," Yurula responded. "It was an honor to assist Soliss in tending Strangers to our village. While you were both asleep earlier this morning, Culil Matroci stopped by. He says that when you are feeling up to it, we would be happy to prepare a feast and celebration in your honor."

"Feast?" Paris perked up considerably. "Sounds wonderful."

Yurula stopped putting things away and regarded him steadily. She went to him, knelt beside him, and pressed her cheek to his forehead. Paris raised an eyebrow and looked at Chakotay. Recalling his own reaction not so long ago when Yurula did this to him, Chakotay grinned. Yes, Tom too was definitely feeling better.

"Let us see how you feel throughout the day," she stated, rising and putting her hands on her hips. "Soliss will not like it if you have a relapse. But if you continue to feel well, I see no reason why we should not have our welcoming celebration. The skywatchers tell us the weather will change after midday and the night should be bright and clear. Perfect for a ceremony. And you two will have to do nothing more strenuous than sit and enjoy yourselves."

"Sounds like a plan," announced Paris. For a moment, Chakotay found himself smiling in anticipation. Then he remembered Yurula's arms filled with the deformed child, taking it to be abandoned to the wild things of this place. Tears on her face, but resolute, confident that she was doing the right thing.

His smile faded, and an ache rose in his chest. There was so much good here, so much kindness. Such talent. And yet, and yet.

He turned back to chopping the vegetables with unnecessary vigor.

Paris continued to improve throughout the afternoon, though he did crawl back to his pallet for a nap at one point. The Culilann skywatchers' forecasting had been completely accurate. As they had predicted, the steady drizzle slowly stopped and the clouds parted, revealing a dazzling blue sky and two suns, one large and one small. Steam rose from the earth as the hot suns baked the moisture out of it.

With evening came a welcome coolness and even a breeze. Soliss had brought some beautiful robes for the humans to wear. "Our finest weaver has been working on these since the day you arrived," he told them.

The garments were a deep indigo hue, comfortingly soft to the touch. They were light and loose-fitting, allowing air to circulate and cool the body, necessary in this hot, damp climate. They sported intricate embroidery with threads of every color of the rainbow. The patterns curled and turned in on themselves, narrowing here, blossoming out there. Jewels had been sewn into the sleeves and flashed in the firelight. Chakotay shrugged into his with ease; it fit perfectly.

"Did you measure us while we were asleep?" he asked in a mock-accusing voice.

Soliss smiled. "Nothing quite that extreme," he said, "but Ramma did come and see you. He's got a very accurate eye for such things."

Paris struggled with the clothing, needing some assistance, but eventually he was able to don it. With his fair skin and blue eyes, he looked striking in the deep purple-blue color. He stood unsteadily, and Soliss gave him a staff. It was made of light-colored wood, polished smooth as a river stone.

"This will help you walk without assistance," said Soliss. "You will not have to walk far."

"Which is a very good thing," said Paris, but he smiled. Chakotay was pleased. They were both well on their way to recovery. Soon, they'd have to think about a way to contact *Voyager*. Chakotay was surprised at how long it had been since the thought of his ship had crossed his mind. Several hours, at the very least. It wasn't paradise here on—whatever planet this was, but it did offer a leisurely pace and a great deal of beauty.

The suns had completely set, and Chakotay saw

shapes scurrying about outside, lighting torches and fires. He could hear their excited conversation and laughter, though he could not understand the words. Among themselves, the Culilann conversed in their own language. It was only to Tom and Chakotay that they spoke Federation Standard. Then, slowly, steadily, the drumming began, and a shudder of deep, primal recognition washed through him.

He knew that every culture on Earth used percussion in ritual at one time or another, depending on its stage of development. He had learned from both study and personal observation that nearly every alien culture that had a noticeable heartbeat also used drums. He was certain that was not a coincidence. Sometimes the drumming had died out; other times, it was part of deeply honored rituals that continued through the centuries. But always he had found that if a species had a heartbeat, it had drums in its blood if you searched far enough.

BOOM-boom-BOOM-boom-BOOM-BOOM-BOOM-boom-BOOM-boom. He already felt his body wanting to move to the primal, steady rhythm. He, the "contrary" one, never at home in any one place. Too modern for the pace of his people, too locked into tradition for a starship commander. It was no different here. He was moved by and responded to many of the traditions of the Culilann, appalled by others.

"Needs a little guitar or Harry's clarinet, but it'll do," said Tom, startling Chakotay out of his reverie.

"They are waiting for you," said Soliss.

"Then let's go," said Tom.

* * *

135

Paris always hated it when he was sick or injured. He felt weak and frail, and his body wouldn't obey simple commands like *stand* or *walk* or *don't throw up*. And he had been very sick, and very badly injured, and his body had totally ignored any commands he'd been well enough to send it for far too long.

Soliss's staff was a thing of beauty and of great practicality. Having tried nearly every sport he'd ever heard of, Paris had done his share of hiking and knew the value of a good, solid staff. He curled his fingers around this one, stood as straight as his body would let him, and concentrated on putting one foot in front of the other as he followed Chakotay out the door. Soliss brought up the rear.

Two men with torches stood at attention outside the door. They turned as smartly as any Academy cadet to escort the two Strangers to the festivities. Paris sniffed the cool night air and caught a whiff of something delicious cooking. Some sort of meat, probably roasting on a spit or in an open pit. His mouth filled with saliva. For the first time in what seemed to be ages, he was very hungry.

The wonderful aromas grew stronger as they walked down the main thoroughfare to where the forested area began. Paris was feeling a bit wobbly again. He ordered his legs to continue to support him, and for the moment they obeyed.

Torches formed a corridor, showing where they should go. The drumming sound grew louder, competing with the other sounds of a jungle at night. They entered the brush, but the path had been meticulously cleared and Paris's unsteady feet didn't stumble. The path opened out into a large clearing.

At their appearance, the drumming stopped. Gathered in the clearing were about eighty people. Paris guessed it was the entire populace of this little village. They looked surreal in the moonlight, their pale blue skin and hair almost glowing. But the unearthly faces wore smiles of welcome.

A young man stepped forward. He seemed to be weighted down by the regalia of some important office, but his movements were smooth and elegant. He raised his arms and spoke first in his native tongue, then in Federation Standard for the benefit of the strangers.

"I, Matroci, the Culil of Sumar-ka, welcome the Strangers. It has been long since the Crafters have sent us new friends who will teach us; new students whom we may teach. We ask their forgiveness for the Ordeal. Know that it is part of our deepest tradition, and know that it was for protection only, and not done in a spirit of hostility."

Soliss leaned over and whispered, "You need to formally forgive us."

Chakotay spoke first. "I forgive Matroci, the Culil of Sumar-ka, and the good people of this village. We have survived your Ordeal and stand ready to befriend you."

He turned to Paris. Paris's tongue cleaved to his throat. He didn't really want to forgive these people in such a formal fashion. He wanted to just drop it, pretend it hadn't happened. At his silence, the smiles faded. They looked concerned, even fearful now.

One woman's eyes filled with tears and she glanced away.

He cleared his throat. "Uh, I too forgive the people of Sumar-ka." It wasn't eloquent, but it would do. A murmur of relief swept through the crowd. At Soliss's gesture, they stepped into the clearing and made for large piles of ferns. Tom needed a little help sitting down, but Soliss was so deft in lending the required aid that Paris felt sure no one had noticed.

The ferns made a very comfortable seat. As soon as the strangers had settled into position, the villagers approached, one by one.

The first was the Culil. He bore a beautifully carved wooden tray filled with delicious-looking fruits and vegetables. An exquisite knife lay in the center, clearly to be used to cut up the delicacies. He placed the tray at their feet.

"I offer you food, to nourish body and spirit," said Matroci. "As long as you dwell with our people, we shall see that you never go hungry." He placed his fingers first on his temples, then on his throat, then on his belly. Paris and Chakotay imitated him. Matroci bowed and stepped aside.

Suddenly before Paris stood the most beautiful woman he thought he'd ever seen. She seemed familiar, and he recalled that this was the young woman who had brought them in to undergo the Ordeal. With her lovely blue features and hair, she might have been sculpted of ice, and Ice Queen probably wouldn't have been a bad nickname to describe her personality, either. In each hand she carried an exquisitely wrought bottle of handblown glass.

"I am Trima, Sa-Culil of Sumar-ka. I offer you wine and water, to nourish body and spirit. As long as you dwell with our people, we shall see that you never go thirsty."

She lowered herself down—*squatted* was far too ugly a word to describe that fluid, graceful movement—and placed the bottles in front of them. Like a silvery blue water spirit rising from a lake, she rose, regarded each of them in turn with piercing blue eyes, and lithely stepped aside. Paris found his eyes following her, and it took the sound of another voice speaking directly to him to make him turn and face forward.

It was Soliss and Yurula, offering medicinal herbs. And then came someone else, carrying between them on a platter a delectable-looking roast something or other. Someone else approached, offering clothing. On and on they came, one after the other, the gifts starting to pile high around him and Chakotay. After the adults came the children, offering trinkets, toys, small pet animals in makeshift cages, beloved things collected in the halcyon hours of childhood. It was overwhelming.

At last, the onslaught of gifts and welcoming was over. The formal mood shattered like glass dropped on a hard floor. A ululating cry of anticipation went up from somewhere in the crowd, and even the sober Culil smiled.

"Now we eat!" he said.

And eat they did. The bounty of the food nearly equaled that of the gifts. Roasted beasts, fish, and fowl were brought for them to partake of. A variety of handmade cups, filled with beverages of varying degrees of potency, were pressed into their hands. Savory soups; crunchy, juicy fruits and vegetables; porridges of grains mixed with fruit pulp and eaten with the fingers; flower-scented sweets that dissolved into heady flavor the instant they were placed on the tongue; all manner of culinary delights were paraded in front of them.

Tom was ravenous and ate as if to make up for the lost—days? weeks?—of illness. He felt his stomach's growling subside as it was first placated, then filled. The skin on his belly was stretched taut by the time he ruefully waved away something made of fruit paste, sweet tubers, and meat that smelled heavenly.

"I can't eat another bite," he said, and it was the honest truth.

Chakotay, too, looked utterly sated. His eyes even seemed a little glazed. But perhaps, thought Tom, that was just the alcohol in his own system talking.

The villagers seemed pleased by the quantity of food that the Strangers had eaten, although to Paris it looked as though they had merely made a dent in the huge mountain of comestibles. The food was taken away and the drumming began again.

"You are welcome to join in our dancing," said Culil Matroci. "You are citizens of Sumar-ka now. You are no longer Strangers."

"That is very kind of you," Chakotay replied. "I can't speak for Mr. Paris, but I'm far too full to dance right now."

The handsome young face turned its inquiring gaze upon Paris. "I'm stuffed," he admitted, "and

I'm still recovering. We'll enjoy watching you, though," he said, and immediately wondered if he had committed a gross faux pas. But Matroci nodded, as if he had expected the response, and turned to his people.

"Our hearts are full. Our bellies are full. The Crafters have been good to us. The fruits ripen on the trees, the beasts fairly leap into our traps and nets to provide us nourishment. Sometimes they ask something of us for their goodness to us. Winnif, rise."

Slowly, the woman who had borne the deformed child stood. Paris watched her closely. From what Chakotay had said, having her child taken from her had devastated her. There was nothing of grief about her now. She stood proudly, a small smile on her face. She looked like a woman who had done something wonderful, and knew it. Those who were seated near her looked up at her with a sort of awe.

"Winnif, you have sacrificed your child unto the care of the gods. They have accepted your offering."

"Truly," said Yulura. "I returned this afternoon to the sacred mountain, and the child had indeed been taken by the Crafters!"

"It is well," said Matroci.

"It is well!" came the full-voiced cry of response.

"At such times as this we dance, to thank the Crafters and to ask for their continued protection against the encroachment of the Alilann." The words were allegedly directed to everyone present, but Paris doubted that the villagers needed to be told what their dancing signified. The explanation was for him and Chakotay.

"For generations we have coexisted peacefully, but the last series of talks and debates with the Alilann went poorly. We owe it to the Crafters not to diminish their importance in our lives by accepting the ways of the Alilann. We will not fight them, but we will stand firm. And when we do, we shall wear garments that are blessed, that will keep us from harm. The Crafters will wash away the Alilann, and we, the Culilann, will remain. Come, let us dance!"

Slowly, with reverence and closed eyes, bodies lost to the motion, the villagers rose and formed a circle around the fire. Suddenly, Chakotay gasped.

"What is it?" asked Paris.

For a long moment Chakotay didn't reply. He stared at the dancers as if transfixed. Then slowly, with pain in his voice he replied, "The Ghost Dance. They're doing the Ghost Dance."

"What's the Ghost Dance?"

Chakotay turned to look at him, his dark eyes picking up the red glint of the flickering flames. "In Earth's nineteenth century, there was a great deal of conflict between the European settlers and the natives of the Americas. There arose a leader named Wovoka, who prophesied that all white men would be swallowed by the Earth, and all dead Indians would emerge and enjoy a world free from their conquerors. It would be a new era for the native peoples. His followers performed something called the Ghost Dance, in honor of the dead who would arise. Participants would dance in a circle, just like this one. Word of the Ghost Dance spread throughout the western part of the United States, and it alarmed the white government."

"Did Wovoka advocate violence?"

"No, quite the opposite. He expressly stated that his followers weren't to make any trouble. But the whites were still worried. The famous Indian chief Sitting Bull was killed because he was believed to be an instigator of an impending rebellion. His followers were rounded up and placed in an encampment near Wounded Knee Creek."

"That sounds familiar," said Paris.

"The Lakota Indians weren't worried. They took the ideals of the Ghost Dance a step further. They made sacred shirts, believed to be bulletproof."

Paris knew about bullets, and he didn't like the way this story was going. "But they weren't bulletproof, were they?" he asked, turning to watch the dancers.

"No," Chakotay replied, his voice soft. "They weren't. In December of 1890, a shot was fired within the camp and the soldiers began shooting. They massacred some two hundred unarmed men, women, and children. Those who tried to escape the battle were pursued and killed. All because of the fear stirred up by the Ghost Dance."

He didn't say anything more. He didn't have to. Paris watched the figures moving in the firelight and desperately hoped that history was not about to repeat itself.

The rain had finally stopped, but slogging along in sopping wet clothes was still far from relaxing in a holosim of a glorious, sunny, *dry* afternoon. But Ioni was used to it, and strode purposefully along. It was their leader, Ezbai, the soft Interceptor, who seemed to be suffering the most.

The tiny bundle in her arms whimpered. She cuddled it close as best she could and made soft noises. They needed to transport, and soon. They had brought nothing that was fit for an infant to eat. But they were still within what was called the forbidden parameter—too close to the primitives to risk utilizing high-level technology. They might be discovered.

The baby was very healthy, and anger again rose inside her. He kicked, and filled his lungs. "No, shh, shh," she urged softly. The cry of an irritated and hungry baby would give them away quicker than the hum of a transporter. The noise pierced her ears. His little body heaved with his wails. As one, the group picked up their pace to a trot. Soon, now, they would be able to transport.

He kicked, angry. His small right foot waved in the air. This was what he had been sentenced to death for, equinus of the ankle, varus of the heel, and adduction of the forefoot—an affliction that would be remedied by a doctor in a matter of minutes.

She hated them.

Dirty, stinking, feebleminded primitives. Why did the Alilann do these recovery missions undercover, sneaking to the sacred mountain, gathering up the children, taking care that they left no trace of footprints? Why not boldly stride in, snatch the helpless children, and force the Culilann to give up their barbaric ways? All the talk of maintaining peace and harmony between the two castes made her sick, never more so than at moments like these, when she clutched the evidence of their barbarism in her hands.

Everyone would be so much better off if the Culilann were all just exterminated.

Everyone.

CHAPTER

12

THERE WAS A LONG SILENCE. FINALLY, TELEK SAID, slowly, "From what we have learned about the Shepherds, I cannot believe that this is either accidental or dangerous."

"That's a pretty big supposition about a race that seems to take delight in jerking us around," growled Torres.

"But they have not, as you put it, jerked us around," Telek continued. "It is we who have been slow in discovering how to utilize their technology. Thus far, the sphere has enabled us to do everything we have asked of it—once we have determined what we need, and how to ask."

A thought occurred to him. "We have been able to

transport dark matter from space, and from inside transportable objects. But we have not yet determined how we are to extract the dark matter from something as large as a ship. And our sensors tell us that every ship out there is riddled with dark matter, to one degree or another."

"The thought had occurred to me," said Torres. "I just wanted to make sure the people were safe first."

"I'm not disputing your priorities, Lieutenant," Telek continued. "We have worked with this alien technology step by step. We extracted dark matter from space, the simplest step. We learned that we needed to utilize the transporter to remove dark matter from living tissue, the next logical step. Now we face a greater challenge—removing it from inside something we cannot dematerialize. Perhaps this field can be useful in that context. Thus far, it does not appear to be harmful. We are doing the Shepherds' bidding in gathering up the dark matter, after all. I fail to see how giving us something that is a danger when used properly would further that goal."

"Well phrased, Dr. R'Mor," said Vorik approvingly. "A brilliant and logical deduction. It is sometimes very obvious that Romulans and Vulcans are descended from the same common ancestor."

Telek knew the young Vulcan meant it as a compliment, but he bridled nonetheless. It was an ingrained, learned response, and he fought his resentment down. Few Romulans liked being reminded of their origins. He needed to remember that, for the time being, everyone on this ship was on the same side.

He noticed that Seven did not appear to be listening. She was busy at the console, checking something. Telek knew, though, that the former Borg had heard and registered every word he said.

"Curious," said Seven. "We know that the sphere is growing every time transporter energy is passed through it. Within the circumference of the field, every trace of dark matter has disappeared. And the amount of dark matter inside our artificial warp bubble has increased point zero zero zero eight percent over what we have registered as being transferred there."

Khala moved forward, craning a long, elegant neck to examine Seven's numbers. "You're right," she said. "And so were you, Telek. The radiation seems to be gathering up dark matter all on its own."

"Let me see that," said Torres, pushing her way in to view it with her own eyes. "My God, it's true. I don't want to try it on people yet, but—Seven, check out the contents of Cargo Bay Two. Identify everything that has dark matter in it."

"That would be fourteen containers of various sizes," said Seven.

"Dematerialize it all. That's more cubic meters than we've tried yet at one time. Separate the dark matter and then return it to the cargo bay. Let's monitor this and see what our field does."

Everyone went to his or her own console. Telek was brimming with excitement. If he was right, if the field increased with the amount of energy fed to the sphere, then the possibilities were almost limitless.

"Energize," ordered Torres.

As before, the orb turned red and made its by-now

familiar, terrible noise. The light was too great for them to see what happened, but the sensors would record it.

Seven could see what transpired and gave them a report. "The field is increasing by one point eight percent. Holding steady. Transport is complete. The dark matter is now inside the sphere."

"Transport to the warp bubble," snapped Torres.

"Transporting," replied Seven.

Again came the sound, the bright red light, and again when the sound and light both faded, the ball was empty and hovering peacefully, its usual serene hue.

Another success. Another—how was it the humans put it?—carrot to dangle before them to encourage them to take the next step, learn the next lesson. If the stakes had not been so high, the situation so dire, Telek would have found this entire thing an exciting exercise.

"The radiation sphere has again increased," said Seven. "The console and the floor area are completely free of dark matter."

Telek's heart was racing. Something about this whole bizarre encounter with *Voyager* and the Shepherds sang to his soul. He was thrilled at the progress they were making, but impatient with the slow speed of the steps. Sometimes, daring and courage were what were called for, and Telek sensed that at this moment.

He stepped forward and lifted his hand, directly into the unseen sphere of radiation.

"Telek!" cried Torres. "You don't know . . ." Her

voice trailed off as she realized it was too late. He smiled at her, a fierce, triumphant smile.

"Seven," he said, "scan me."

Even she looked uneasy at his unpredictable and perhaps dangerously impulsive move, but she obeyed his request. Her thin golden eyebrows lifted in surprise.

"There is no reaction, negative or positive. You appear to remain undamaged, Dr. R'Mor, but the sphere is not activating to draw dark matter out of your system."

"He's already been purged," said Khala. "We need to expose someone who hasn't already been transported."

Torres tapped her combadge. "Engineering to bridge."

"Janeway here," came the captain's voice.

"We're making a great deal of progress, Captain, but we need a guinea pig. Someone who hasn't been materialized and had the dark matter removed from his system."

There was a pause. "I'm coming down."

"Captain, I—"

"Don't even try, Torres. You're in need of a test subject, I'm in need of having this stuff removed from my tissues. On my way."

Torres glanced up, frustration, irritation, and helplessness written plainly on her features. Clearly, trying this on the captain wasn't exactly what she had in mind.

A few moments later, the door hissed open and Janeway strode in. She looked excited, as excited as

Telek had felt when he had, perhaps foolishly, exposed himself to the radiation. Briefly, Torres explained the situation. Janeway, trained scientist that she was, grasped it perfectly and nodded her understanding. Seven stepped up and scanned her right arm with the tricorder.

"You are free of large concentrations of dark matter," said Seven, "but there are minute traces in the phalange of your thumb and in the lunate carpal. It will be sufficient for the testing requirements. You may proceed."

"Thank you," said Janeway, with a hint of amusement. Then, calmly, she placed her hand where Torres had indicated.

When Telek had done so earlier, the orb and the field had not reacted. This time, the orb lit up in its by-now recognizable fashion and emitted the screeching sound. Janeway, for whom all of this was a new experience, looked somewhat concerned in the brief instant before the light grew too bright for Telek to look.

When the light and sound had died, they all turned excitedly to Seven.

"The dark matter has not been removed from the phalange and lunate carpal," she announced. She looked disappointed. "However, Captain, you appear to be undamaged."

"Well," said Janeway gamely, "that's something."

"I don't understand," said Khala suddenly. "This ought to have worked. The orb reacted, it tried to take the dark matter out of the captain's hand. It's the next logical step. What is the field for if not to aid in the recovery of dark matter?"

"It does," said Seven. "We have been able to ascertain that all dark matter within its circumference was transported first to the orb and then to the warp bubble."

"All dark matter save that which is within living tissue," said Janeway thoughtfully. "It might be a safety measure of some sort."

"Too bad we don't have a real guinea pig," said Torres. "It would be nice to have a test subject other than a humanoid."

"Living tissue," said Janeway again. "Ensign Vorik, go to the aeroponics bay. Take your tricorder and scan the plants there for traces of dark matter. If you find any, bring them back here at once."

Vorik nodded and left immediately. Telek understood what Janeway was driving at. Plants had their own complexities, to be sure, but they weren't as complex as humanoids. Maybe the sphere would work on them.

Now, for perhaps the first time, the true scope of the task they had been set dawned on him. They would have to remove dark matter not only from space and from individuals. They would have to remove it from ships, from plants—from planets. From stars. From solar systems, perhaps. True, not every person or plant on every planet would be contaminated. In fact, the odds were that only a small percentage of dark matter would be present any time it was detected. Still, when one considered the vastness of space, it was a daunting task.

And the tiny, purple, floating orb was their only tool.

Vorik returned, carrying a tray with three plants of varying sizes. Torres appropriated them at once. "Seven," she asked, "is the radiation still present?"

"Affirmative, though it is slowly decreasing."

Carefully, holding the tray firmly, Torres extended it toward the sphere and held it there.

"The plants are within the radiation's—" began Seven, but the terrible noise and bright red light interrupted her. When they had faded, she checked the computer.

"The dark matter has been removed from all three of the plants," she said.

"Do you realize what this means?" said Telek, unable to control himself. "Captain, we can extract dark matter from anything now—plants, people, ships, even planets! All we need to do is to increase the size of the radiation sphere!"

"It's a good beginning," said Janeway, placing a cautioning hand on Telek's shoulder. "But we're far from being able to sweep entire planets clean."

"The transporter was operating at maximum capacity, and we were only able to increase it a little over a meter," added Torres, somewhat glumly.

Janeway's keen blue eyes examined each of them in turn. "Unless I'm greatly mistaken, we're well into the second shift. That means all of you are off duty."

They all protested at once. Janeway raised her hands, smiling. Her decision had been made. "Right now, it's going to take several more hours' worth of work before we've even transported the crews of the Kwaisi ships. The second shift should be able to handle that without a problem."

The door hissed open just as she was speaking. Harry Kim entered. He smiled when he met Khala's eyes. "I must agree with the captain," he said. "Khala, will you join me for dinner?"

Khala looked from Harry to Torres to Janeway. "You'll be back at work first thing in the morning, I assure you," said Janeway. "Because, like Dr. R'Mor, I too am looking forward to being able to rid entire planets of dark matter at a single go. In the meantime, eat something and go to bed. You all look exhausted."

It was nothing less than the truth. Telek could not see himself, but he could feel the strain in his shoulders and neck from the constant tension, could sense how bloodshot-green his eyes must be after hours with no breaks.

The crew exchanged glances, then silently headed for the door.

Harry had spent an entire hour wondering what to do for dinner with Khala. Should he program the holodeck? Khala might enjoy the slightly run-down but cozy atmosphere of Sandrine's, or the laid-back milieu of Polynesian resort simulation three. Perhaps she'd like a picnic on a ship aboard the Black Sea at night, or maybe Lake George, or Lake Como.

Or he could simply prepare a repast in his quarters. In the end, that was what he had opted to do. He didn't know Khala well enough to know what her likes and dislikes were, and didn't want to risk offending her with the wrong holodeck program.

Of course, though, the minute she appeared at his

door, he frantically wished he had opted for the holodeck. "Come," he called.

She had replicated a dress for the occasion, and looked almost as awkward as Harry felt. "Is this all right? I mean, is it appropriate? I asked Seven about it, and she told me to ask the Doctor, and this was what he suggested . . ."

Her voice trailed off at Harry's silence. "I'm sorry. Let me go back and change—"

"Oh, don't," said Harry, earnestly.

He was silent because he was stunned at how truly beautiful Khala was. She had been lovely in her uniform, of course; beauty shines through no matter what costume it wears. But she stood before him now, hair freshly washed and combed, replicated sapphires sparkling at her ears and throat. The dress she wore was a symphony of soft pastel shades of white, blue, silver, indigo, and purple. It draped one shoulder, leaving the other sky-blue shoulder bare. A silver belt emphasized a small waist, and simple blue slippers completed the outfit.

"You look . . ." He fumbled for words. "You look amazing." Not it was his turn to feel uncomfortable. "I didn't know you were going to dress up, or I'd have—"

"Oh, Harry, I didn't want to—"

Their eyes met and suddenly they both laughed. "Okay," said Harry, "You look gorgeous, I look like a boring old Starfleet ensign, but I am going to make you a wonderful dinner so you'll forgive me."

She relaxed, the smile spreading across her face and lighting up her eyes. "Sounds wonderful. I haven't had anything since lunch, and that was hours ago."

"Please sit down," he said, indicating the sofa. "Computer, two glasses and a bottle of 2063 Dom Pérignon champagne." He took the bottle and glasses and sat down beside her, handing her a glass.

"This isn't the real stuff, of course, but it's pretty good synthehol," he said, and then winced. Once again, he'd insulted Khala's choice of artificial over real. Rushing on, he poured them each a generous amount of the sparkling beverage, and said, "To the success of our quest: to finding every last piece of dark matter and getting rid of the stuff!"

She laughed brightly. "I will definitely drink to that."

The synthehol was good, and Harry continued preparing the meal. He had decided to expose Khala to a wide variety of dishes to see which she favored. With the replicator, there was no waste. Anything they didn't eat went right back in.

He started with antipasti, a dish from Earth's Italy. Khala seemed to enjoy the tart flavors of olives, cheeses, and roasted peppers. She was less fond of the algae puffs and *plomeek* soup, but, to Harry's amazement, she devoured the Owon eggs and *hasperat* with gusto.

He finished up with a simple chocolate cake and Vulcan spiced tea. Khala accepted the cup and brought it to her nose. She sniffed and smiled.

"Mmmm, that smells wonderful," she said. She took a sip. "And it's so delicious! Harry, thank you so much for all of this. You've been so kind to me."

"Aw, shucks, ma'am, 'tweren't nothing," he drawled.

"No, really." She moved closer to him and gently placed a hand on his knee. "I don't know why I was brought here, but you've made it easier for me. Being able to contribute helps, too, but the time when I'm not actually working, well . . . it could be awfully lonely."

He looked at her for a long moment. "I can't imagine you ever being lonely," he said. "You probably have to beat the men off with a stick."

"Me?" She looked genuinely surprised. "Oh, no. I'm a pretty solitary person, actually. When I do spend time with someone, it's usually my family."

"Tell me about them."

She did so, and Harry learned of a brilliant but self-conscious older brother, a fussy but loving mother, and a slightly distant father who was nonetheless clearly proud of his two intelligent offspring.

"Tell me more about this interceptor bit," said Harry.

"Well, as I told you earlier, sometimes alien races don't contact us, they contact the Culilann. We have interceptors who try to catch these poor aliens who fall through the cracks before they reach the Culilann. Once they have made contact, though, it becomes the field team's responsibility. They have to conduct a recovery—go out and find and bring back the aliens."

"So that's what your brother Ezbai does? He leads these missions?"

She threw back her head and laughed at that. "Oh, no, not Ezbai. You'd never see anyone more out of his element than Ezbai three meters into the jungle. No, he is well suited to the job of interceptor, which means he monitors things and tells *other* people to go out into the rain forest and recover the aliens and the infants."

"Infants? You lost me."

She wrinkled her adorable little nose, and Harry knew he was in for another diatribe against the Culilann. "They are so primitive," she sighed. "Any child who is born deformed is exposed—left at their so-called sacred mountain for their fictitious gods to rescue."

"They abandon their children to die in the elements?" Harry was truly horrified at this. His imaginative mind raced with all the dreadful possibilities.

"They would if it weren't for us," declared Khala. "We have a spy planted in each village who notifies us when this happens, and we send out the emergency recovery teams at once. We can get to the infant within an hour at the outside. We take them in, cure whatever it was that so offended the Culilann about them, and raise them as Alilann children."

Kim found this admirable. "That's awfully nice of you."

"Well, we couldn't just let them die, could we? We'd be just like the Culilann then."

"But the Culilann don't think they're leaving them to die, and honestly, you're playing right into their false thinking. The children *are* always taken away by some benevolent being. It's just that instead of the Crafters, it's their own kind."

"We are not the same kind!" exclaimed Khala. "Haven't you heard a word I've said?"

This was not the way Harry had wanted the evening to go. "I understand they're a different caste, but you're the same race. You even raise their children to be Alilann."

Khala sighed, calming somewhat. "I'm sorry I snapped at you, Harry. It must be so hard for you to understand this, coming from a different culture. Infants are one thing. We raise them Alilann, and Alilann they are. But older children, adults—they are Culilann to their bones. And I understand you better than I understand them."

Harry was silent. "Let me tell you about my family," he said. He told her of being raised as the golden child, the only offspring of elderly parents. He spoke of his love for them, the closeness he felt, and how awful it was, even after all this time in the Delta Quadrant, to be separated from them. And finally, his heart racing and his palms wet, he told her about the clarinet.

"Clarinet? What is that?"

"It's a musical instrument," he said. Rising, he went to retrieve it. "I replicated it early on in the voyage, so that I could stay in practice."

Still she did not understand. "Instrument? Is it then a diagnostic tool of some sort?"

He licked dry lips. "No, it makes music."

"You are using all kinds of words that are unfamiliar to me," she said, laughing. "Show me what this does."

Harry stared. She didn't even know what music

was. He had imagined that there was at least some kind of corollary in her regimented, precisely controlled world, perhaps tunes composed by computer. But apparently there was nothing.

He swallowed hard. Lifting the clarinet to his lips, he began to play.

Khala started at the sound. Her lovely face registered puzzlement, then confusion, then something akin to panic.

"Stop it," she said.

He ceased playing. "What's wrong?" He had an idea, of course, but wanted to hear her put it into words.

"You are making rhythmic sound from it," she said, edging away from him. "The Culilann do that. It's forbidden."

"We eat fresh-grown foods, and create art and music and poetry," said Kim, pushing his point frantically. "But we build starships and understand warp drive and sometimes listen to artificially constructed music, too. It's okay, Khala."

"No. No it's not. It's—it's wrong, Harry. It's sick. Excuse me, I have to go." She turned and hastened out, but not before he saw tears glistening in her beautiful sapphire eyes.

Harry's stomach was knotted. He wondered if he'd be able to keep dinner down. She couldn't have hurt him worse if she'd tried, and he knew that her reaction was something she couldn't help. But oh, God, the look on her face, as if he were doing something terrible just by playing the clarinet.

Music had been the constant love of Harry's life.

It had kept him sane and comforted during the separation from his parents, from Libby, during the wrenching agony of his relationship with the Varro woman Tal, during the long trip into the Void. It was his touchstone. No one could be close to him without accepting and understanding the call that playing the clarinet had on his soul.

Khala thought playing music was sick, was wrong. He knew it wasn't. It was something he'd always been proud of, was good at—something he did that other people enjoyed and admired. In many ways, he was his music.

He lay down on the bed and curled up with his clarinet. The shame and pain that washed through him told him all he needed to know. Harry Kim was falling in love with a woman to whom the most precious thing in his life was an abomination.

And he couldn't stop it.

INTERLUDE

THE PLANET THE ENTITY APPROACHED WAS STILL LUSH and fertile. It was not almost dead, as that of the Baneans had been. There was not much dark matter here to be collected, but as it drew closer, the Entity realized that there did not need to be much for dreadful damage to be done.

It settled down, an invisible cloud, and brushed lovingly across the surface of an ocean, of forests, of beautiful, graceful buildings. A molecule here, a few more there. And then there was the darkness.

It had not ravaged the man's body, nor his mind. It was something else that had been broken and twisted, something some spiritual peoples called a "soul." Almost the Entity recoiled from the man, and in so doing learned something about itself: it was inherently good.

Resolute, it moved toward the man. His name was Gath. He had once held a high rank among his people, the Sikarians. More information came to the Entity, though somehow the knowledge was already familiar. Gath had once been what was called a minister. The Sikarians were famed for their hospitality, though even before the coming of the wrong things the Entity sensed that this "hospitality" had been self-serving. The Sikarians lived for amusement and pleasure, and all too quickly they grew tired of something that had once entertained them.

Such was still the Sikarian way, the Entity sensed, but in Gath, the drive for pleasure had been perverted. Gath obtained his pleasure from the pain of others. Once he had been thoughtless and lacked compassion. Now he was cruel. Evil. The dark matter inside him had made him so.

The woman who had given him so much pleasure earlier that evening now lay sobbing in another room. She bore bruises and burns and cuts. Perhaps a bone or two had been broken. Gath did not care. Her sobs annoyed him. Already, the pleasure that had filled him at her suffering was fading, and he was thinking of what else he could do to the girl to rejuvenate his interest in her. He had never killed, but now that he thought of it. . . .

Horror and anger racked the Entity. This must be stopped. The Entity could not prevent the damage Gath had done, but it felt certain that it could stop future wrongs. It descended, unseen by Gath, and gently swept through him.

Gath gasped. His body tingled. He felt as if he were on fire. The pain, the pain . . . ! And then it was gone. He stared at the blood still on his hands, and the blood stains on his robes.

"What have I done?" he whispered, but he knew. He remembered everything. Remorse welled inside him, an alien sensation, but one he embraced like a drowning man might a lifeline. He rushed into the room, where the broken girl shrieked and cringed away from him.

"Mirta, please, please forgive me. I don't know why I did these awful things to you. I am so sorry. Here, let me take you to a doctor."

There were a few stray bits to gather on this planet: dark matter that had killed an ancient tree, that had turned a fresh rivulet into poison. The Entity found them all. With a sense of deep satisfaction, it moved on.

CHAPTER
13

JEKRI FOUND, TO HER SURPRISE, THAT IT WAS DIFFICULT to be her old self in front of her crew. For the last few weeks, she had been practicing the Vulcan mental disciplines that Dammik R'Kel had taught her. She had achieved a sense of inner calm that dampened her normal fire. Things did not irritate her as they used to, and she had to put on a show of snapping and growing irate at small errors.

While she was pleased that there was a definite effect from her meditating, she did not know if the most important aspect had succeeded. Until someone tried to read her thoughts, she would not know if her mental blocks were effective.

No one had suspected anything. Jekri answered to

no one save the Praetor and the Empress. The Praetor, who appeared, at least, to still be an ally, had done nothing to contact her, and the Empress—

Jekri frowned as she sat at her console. This, at least, she did not have to feign. As chairman of the Tal Shiar, little was withheld from her. There was the occasional clash between her offices and that of the military, but more often than not she was the victor in such confrontations. Now, however, she was looking at an encrypted message that had been intercepted a few hours ago. It was not one of the dozen or so codes with which she was familiar.

"Kaleh to Sharibor," she said tapping her communications badge.

"Sharibor here, Chairman."

"Which do you value less, your job or your life? Because I am inclined to eliminate one or the other at the present moment. I'm in a good mood, so I'll give you your choice." She was joking, of course, but only by a hair.

"Chairman?"

"I have before me an encrypted message. I can't even determine who sent it or to whom it was sent. Are you not my chief of decoding?"

An uncomfortable pause. "My entire team has spent the last few hours on this, Chairman. I passed it along to you in the hopes that you might have an insight that we lacked."

Fury rose in Jekri like a red wave. Almost at once, the mantra she had learned at Dammik's feet came into her mind: *Anger serves no master. Tame it, and control it.* She didn't want to. Jekri kept her position through skill and intimidation. But other words Dammik spoke came to her.

We can begin with this—controlling your outbursts. I imagine such a skill would be extremely useful to the chairman of the Tal Shiar.

My temper is under my control.

Perhaps, when you deem it to be useful. Perhaps when you are negotiating with an ambassador, or the Praetor, or the Empress, you can control what you say and how you behave. But you must learn to control it at all times. You must not insult a child whose plaything has made you trip, or a servant who has prepared the wrong food.

Or, thought Jekri now, *a loyal underling who has tried but failed.*

"In the future, Sharibor," she said, her voice calm, "I wish to be notified. I do not wish to be surprised with this information and your lack of progress."

"Certainly, Chairman." Jekri wasn't certain, but she thought she detected a note of relief in Sharibor's voice.

"I will notify Subcommander Verrak. We will meet you at your station. Perhaps more brains working on this puzzle will solve it."

"As you will, Chairman." Yes, it was there, a definite lightness in the voice. Sharibor was married and had children. She could ill afford to have all opportunities barred to her, as would certainly be the case if she were abruptly removed from such a sensitive position.

In a few moments, Jekri was at the encryption station. Most Romulan vessels had one, but on such vessels as warbirds they were smaller and manned by only a few soldiers. It was a subdivision of communications/operations. Here, on the personal vessel of the chairman of the Tal Shiar, it was a huge station. It comprised almost a full level and had some of the finest brains in the Empire. There were over two dozen Romulans stationed here at any given time, more during sensitive missions or whenever Jekri felt they were needed. Now, there were thirty-five warm bodies on duty.

Sharibor Krel was their head, a large, awkward female who had a bit of a reputation for clumsiness, but whose fingers flew over a console and whose mind was as brilliant as any Jekri had ever encountered, up to and including the missing Telek R'Mor and the hated Lhiau. Jekri had once confided to Verrak that she would rather have Sharibor and a primitive calculating device than the finest computers the Empire could provide. Something that was thwarting her and her entire team was something Jekri needed to know about, and fast.

Sharibor rose quickly at the approach of her commander—too quickly, for she slammed her elbow into the console. She closed her eyes briefly against the pain.

"Chairman, I ask your forgiveness." Sharibor spread her hands, nearly missing a cup she had placed on the console. "I am unaccustomed to failure and did not know how to properly react."

That, Jekri could well believe. "I cannot remember the last time you failed me, Sharibor," she said generously.

Sharibor's curved eyebrows rose in surprise at the

calm reaction. She glanced at Verrak, who had come up quietly behind his commander, and then at Jekri, and decided not to pursue the matter.

Instead, she took them both through the lengthy process the encryption had undergone. Sharibor knew off the top of her head over forty-seven different encryptions. The technology that graced the *Tektral* was the best to be found in the Empire. Sharibor's staff ranged from an elderly man who sometimes confounded enemies by utilizing codes that had been deciphered and, therefore, forgotten decades ago to fresh-faced top graduates of the various Romulan academies. Most encrypted messages were decoded with a casualness that would shock those who sent them.

This one, though, remained elusive. Jekri watched the letters, in no language she understood, curl across the screen.

"There is no pattern, no recognizable language, nothing. We might as well be looking at a message from a completely alien race," said Sharibor in her deep, gruff voice.

"Any hint as to the origin?"

"No. We traced it back through three separate routes before the signal degraded."

Jekri's hours of meditation had sharpened her senses even as they had given her clues on how to calm her sometimes raging emotions. She had always trusted her hunches, and everything inside her screamed that this pointed to Lhiau, somehow, some way.

She straightened and looked Verrak in the eye. "It has something to do with Lhiau," she stated.

Verrak glanced down, uncomfortable with her bald statement. "Chairman," he said, "we all know that you have reason to dislike Lhiau. However, perhaps it is not wise to assume that every problem we encounter is caused directly by him."

"On the contrary, Second," said Jekri, her voice sharp, "I have every reason to look first to Lhiau if there is trouble. The Empress has changed her policy radically." Jekri stopped just short of mentioning the Empress's recent bizarre behavior. Such things could be construed as treason among her enemies, and Jekri was hardly *veruul* enough to assume that her vessel was free of those who would make their personal fortunes by trampling over her.

"It may indeed be that R'Mor's wormholes were responsible for the destruction of the fleet. But until we know for certain, it is entirely in keeping with Romulan law and custom that we assume outsiders are the troublemakers, not our own people. Sharibor, have you attempted to cross-reference the signals emitted by Shepherd technology with the signal of this obstinate message?"

Sharibor blushed green. "No, Chairman. I had not. The Shepherds are our allies. I thought—"

"The Earthers are fond of sayings, Sharibor. Some of them even make sense. One of them says to keep your friends close, and your enemies closer. This to me is wisdom. I would have Lhiau suckling at my breast like a newborn babe if I thought it would help me keep watch on him. Now, set your team to this task, and report to me if you find anything. Report to me if you *don't*. Have I made my wishes clear?"

"Perfectly clear, Chairman," said Sharibor stiffly. There was more than a touch of the idealist about the homely Sharibor, despite the cynical nature of her job. It obviously rankled to consider Lhiau, who was posturing as the savior of the Empire, under suspicion.

For the briefest of moments, this troubled Jekri. Then she hardened her will. Sharibor was under her command. She would do what Jekri told her to do. Such was ever the Romulan way.

She turned and strode toward the turbolift. Verrak fell into step beside her. She sensed his disapproval, but he said nothing until they entered the lift.

"Deck seventeen," she told it, and it hummed into motion.

"Permission to speak freely?"

"Granted."

"There is no one who understands your reasons for distrusting Lhiau more than I," said Verrak earnestly. "And you know that I share your distrust. But he is the Empire's ally and the Empress's special favorite at the moment. Do you think it is wise to set yourself against him so openly?"

The anger, the old familiar friend, rose again inside Jekri, but its heat was cooled by Verrak's undeniable logic.

"No," Jekri said, surprising them both with the word. "You are correct. It is not wise to draw such unwanted attention to myself. Thank you for your caution, Second. I shall be more discreet in the future."

He stared at her as the floors rushed by. "Again, if I may speak freely?" At her nod, he continued.

"Chairman, you are different. You hide it well enough from the rest of the crew, but I have served with you far too long not to notice. Do you know something you have not shared with me?"

She could hear it, if she listened for it: the faintest hint of pain that she would keep something from him, from the one who knew her best and served her wholeheartedly. She did not wish to hear, to acknowledge his hurt.

"You are not privy to the innermost thoughts of my mind," she said. "Not you, not Lhiau, no one. You know what I wish you to know, when I wish you to know it."

He stiffened slightly, the old mask of studied indifference dropping into place. "Of course, Honored Chairman."

"Although," she said, though she did not know why she felt compelled to speak, "you do know me better than anyone. And there are things that I have shared with you that I have shared with no one else. Know that, my old friend, and be content."

"I am content," he said, though she knew he lied.

They rode in silence the rest of the way.

Jekri stared at the burning flame of the oil lamp. She sat with her legs crossed, her hands quiet in her lap. Her eyes unfocused, letting the flame lose its distinct shape and become a blur of orange, red, and yellow.

Look within the flame. She could almost hear Dammik's soft voice in her ear. *Look and see not its form, but its essence. See the heat, the passion that is fire. Know it, and take its strength for yourself. Harness fire.*

The chime at her door caused her heart to leap into her throat. She had been utterly lost in the fire meditation, and it took her an entire second or two to recover her composure. With a quick breath, she extinguished the flame and rose. At her touch, the door hissed open.

Sharibor stood there, looking as wretched as Jekri had ever seen her. "Permission to enter?"

Nodding, Jekri stood aside and let her pass. Sharibor's gaze fell briefly on the still smoking lamp, but she said nothing. Jekri wondered if she suspected anything. More likely, Sharibor was surprised to find her icy commander in possession of something as romantically old-fashioned as an oil lamp.

"I assume you have deciphered the encryption?"

Mute, Sharibor nodded and handed her commander a personal data pad.

Jekri inhaled swiftly, the calm she had briefly grasped from the fire meditation fleeing. She had been right. Lhiau had been the author of the message, and he had issued it from the royal palace, with the full knowledge and blessings of the bewitched Empress. It was to the highest levels of the military and, she saw to her horror, to her own people.

Quickly, she read. *The glory and final triumph of the Romulan Empire is in jeopardy. Even as we are positioning our warbirds along the Neutral Zone, preparing for the surprise onslaught of a slow-witted Federation, there is a traitor in our midst. We do not wish to startle the populace, so the instructions that follow are highly classified. The chairman of the Tal Shiar, Jekri Kaleh—*

Sharibor moved in utter silence, strange for one normally so clumsy. There was no revealing scrape of boot on floor, no shadow falling over Jekri to alert her. But her senses were already finely honed, and the meditation she had just completed had left her subconscious alert.

Jekri whirled, knocking the disruptor out of Sharibor's hand with a swift kick. Quick as a snake, faster than Jekri had ever seen the large woman move, Sharibor lunged forward with a *kaleh* that must have been hidden behind her back. It was already in her right hand, arcing toward her belly in a professional underhand stroke by the time Jekri's foot hit the ground from her kick. She sprang back and fancied she could hear a whizzing sound as the knife barely passed her abdomen.

Jekri rushed her attacker as Sharibor stabbed at her again. She seized Sharibor's right hand and bent the wrist up sharply. Jekri slammed her right hand into the inside of Sharibor's wrist. The pain would be agonizing, but Sharibor uttered no sound, not even a wordless hiss. Still, the knife fell from her grasp.

Using her momentum, Jekri slammed her small body into Sharibor's large, muscular one, pinning the larger woman against the bulkhead. Before Sharibor could recover, Jekri had stepped under Sharibor's right arm, which she still clutched, whirled the assassin around and yanked her arm up behind her back.

What she did next startled her. Her left hand came

up, as if it had a will of its own, and clamped down on the side of Sharibor's neck. Fingers placed themselves in proper alignment and she squeezed. Silently, Jekri's would-be assassin dropped to the floor unconscious.

Shaking and breathing heavily, Jekri stared. She had not had the faintest inkling that Sharibor was a plant. The woman had served Jekri with apparent loyalty for many years. She had perfectly played her role of bulky, gawky intellectual, deflecting any suspicion as easily as she might a victim's attack. But she had been well trained—trained the way Jekri herself had been trained. Trained as a professional assassin, a member of the Family of the Blade, planted deeply, awaiting an order that might come any day, or might never come at all.

Veruul! She cried silently. *How could you not have seen it?* The answer came swiftly: for the same reason Jekri's own victims, years ago, had never seen it in her. Oh, Sharibor was good, very good, there was no doubt about it. And yet Jekri was the one still standing, though her knees felt weak. She had triumphed.

Part of her victory was her own training and instincts, but she could not deny how significant a role her Vulcan meditations and exercises had played in her being able to escape with her life. She had foolishly turned her back on Sharibor to read the decoded message and would never have seen the attack coming. One gentle squeeze of a finger on the trigger of the disruptor and Jekri Kaleh would no longer be a problem to anyone.

But her mind had been alert, fresh from her meditation; her fingers had automatically formed themselves into the right position to deliver the famous Vulcan nerve pinch. She recalled practicing it at Dammik's, never being able to get it quite right. But when she had needed it, her subconscious had taken over and had literally saved her life.

Maybe those Vulcans were on to something.

She took a deep, steadying breath and went to her closet to search for something with which to bind her prisoner. She was glad that she had used the nerve pinch instead of killing Sharibor outright. Maybe they would be able to get some useful information out of her before they killed her.

She emerged with a sash from a formal dress she seldom wore. Jekri wrinkled her nose at the flimsiness of the material, but it would have to serve. Quickly she trussed up the unconscious Sharibor. Standing over her, the rage and shame at having been duped the same way she had duped others won out over her newly acquired Vulcan calm, and Jekri kicked Sharibor in the belly. Hard.

She touched her communications device with one hand as she removed her own disruptor. "Kaleh to Verrak."

"Here, Chairman."

"Come to my quarters."

"At once, Chairman."

For not the first time, Jekri was glad of the false affair she and Verrak were pretending to have. Now, when they heard this command, her crew would merely exchange knowing glances among themselves. Before, Jekri's request would have drawn unwanted attention.

Only a few minutes passed before Jekri heard the chime at her door. Keeping the disruptor trained on Sharibor, she went to the door and touched it. It hissed open and she pulled Verrak inside before he could see what was on the floor in her quarters.

He gasped when he saw the prone figure of Sharibor and turned a questioning face to his commander.

"Family of the Blade," Jekri spat. "I should have realized it years ago, but they trained her well."

"Apparently not as well as they trained you," said Verrak admiringly. He reached to touch her face, as if to reassure himself that she was all right, but Jekri stepped quickly away.

"Is she dead?"

"No, just unconscious. Watch her while I finish reading this." She snorted. "She was a good assassin, but she was also a good code breaker."

She finished reading the message that Sharibor had decoded—or perhaps had not decoded, but had already known about. That would be a useful bit of information.

The glory and final triumph of the Romulan Empire is in jeopardy. Even as we are positioning our warbirds along the Neutral Zone, preparing for the surprise onslaught of a slow-witted Federation, there is a traitor in our midst. We do not wish to startle the populace, so the instructions that follow are highly classified. The chairman of the Tal Shiar, Jekri Kaleh, is to be eliminated as a dangerous element. Care is to be utilized. It must not be done in a public setting, and there must be no arousal of suspicion. Disposal of the body should be thorough.

Jekri felt the hairs at the back of her neck prickle. She continued reading.

The first to succeed in this mission shall receive a commendation, monetary compensation, and the gratitude of the Empress.

"No," Jekri whispered, then bit her lip hard to keep further sounds from escaping. She could not believe it. Not the Empress. She was bold, fearless, she would not need to send a secret command to assassins with this sly order. If she wanted Jekri dead, the Empress would arrange a public execution and make sure Jekri suffered shame as well as death. She would not merely arrange a knife in the back. This whole thing reeked of Lhiau.

Wordlessly, she handed it to her Second, then strode to stand over the prone figure of Sharibor. She heard the swift intake of breath and was glad she was not watching Verrak's reactions. Though he tried to hide his emotions, they would be naked on his face now, as they were naked on hers.

"Why did she even bring this to my attention?" Jekri wondered aloud. "Why notify me about this code that she and her team supposedly couldn't break?" Her mind went back to the conversation: *"I have before me an encrypted message. I can't even determine who sent it or to whom it was sent. Are you not my chief of decoding?"*

An uncomfortable pause. *"My entire team has spent the last few hours on this, Chairman. I passed it along to you in the hopes that you might have an insight that we lacked."*

It had made sense at the time, when Jekri trusted Sharibor and had given in to anger and irritation. It made no sense now. It was a violation of regulated procedure, an uncharacteristic lapse on Sharibor's part. And Jekri was willing to bet her life that Sharibor did not permit lapses.

She turned to Verrak, who was attempting to compose himself. "Someone was trying to warn me," she told him. "Someone brought that message to my attention. She would never have told me otherwise."

"Is your unknown ally on the ship or elsewhere?" asked Verrak. "We can try to trace it—"

"There is no point," came Sharibor's voice, dripping scorn. "Whoever it is is too clever, or else it never would have gotten past me."

Jekri whirled. "You will tell me all you know of this, or you will suffer terribly."

Sharibor's face was unrecognizable. Gone was the constant expression of faint anxiety and insecurity. Hatred blazed out of ice-blue eyes, and a faint smile of contempt curled her lip.

All at once Jekri realized she had slipped. She was getting soft, becoming too Vulcan, losing her Romulan edge. She sprang onto Sharibor's body, frantically searching for something she ought to have located the minute Sharibor crumpled to the floor. In her day, it was placed in the sleeve . . . others preferred it in the boot. . . .

A soft crunching sound made her heart contract. "No," she cried, lunging for Sharibor's mouth and wrestling it open. "No, curse you, you will not escape me so easily!"

But already the light in Sharibor's angry eyes was fading. The philotostan chip, a piece of equipment as necessary to a member of the Family as the means with which to dispose of the target, had been located inside Sharibor's mouth. The poison acted quickly, too quickly for Jekri to intervene.

She shook the corpse angrily, cursing. They needed the information housed inside Sharibor's skull. Who was her contact? Who had sent this message? Who else had received it? How many others were planning to succeed where Sharibor had failed?

Gently, Verrak's hand closed on her shoulder. "There is nothing to be gleaned from the dead," he said. "We must focus on the living."

He was right, of course, and Jekri knew it. Still, she gazed at the still, dead face of someone she thought she could trust, and wondered how many other faces she knew smiled and showed obedience, feigned friendship or respect or fear, but were merely masks that hid the iciness of murderous intent.

CHAPTER

14

WHEN CHAKOTAY OPENED HIS SLEEPING EYES ONTO THE searingly bright, yellow, desert landscape, he groaned inwardly. This was becoming all **too** familiar. Where was his true animal teacher, she whom he loved with a special devotion, who was wry and gentle and delicate and so strong that she took his breath away?

"On shore leave, or the spiritual equivalent," came the hateful Q-like voice. "We can't all be on call all the time, you know."

Coyote sat beside a cliché cactus, lifted his head, and howled. Annoyance rose inside Chakotay.

"Please go away," he said.

"What? I am here for your betterment, Ebenezer, to see that you do not walk the path that Jacob Marley—whoops, wrong morality play." He pranced a little, huffily, and fixed Chakotay with piercing yellow eyes.

"You are a figment of my imagination. I have no idea why you have been sent to bother me."

Coyote half-closed his eyes. A pink tongue lolled. He looked like he was laughing. Abruptly, he shut his jaws with a snap and rose on his hind legs. He grew, changed, and developed a human torso. Kneeling, he scooped up some sand with paws that abruptly sprouted four fingers and an opposable thumb. Humming a little under his breath, Coyote shaped the sand into a crude approximation of a human figure.

Chakotay watched intently, all his dislike of the Trickster gone. Something important was transpiring here. He still didn't know why Coyote was coming to him in dreams and visions, but he was going to pay attention, just in case.

"Some say man was made out of clay," said Coyote in a singsong voice. "Some say that Coyote created him, just like this, to trick the other animals. Others say he was crafted from stardust." He fixed Chakotay with those yellow eyes. "Or planted on Earth, a sort of seed from another world. Who knows the real truth? Coyote does, Coyote does!"

He fiddled with his sand man, scraping a few grains here, packing some in there. "Whoops," he said, "got a little dark sand right here. Let's get rid of it, shall we?" With a pointed forefinger, he touched the sand man's head. It crumbled at his touch, followed by the rest of the body.

Coyote blew on the pile of sand in his palm. It

flew up into a dust devil and launched itself at Chakotay's face, stinging his eyes.

He gasped and found himself awake, safe inside the little hut that the Culilann had constructed for him and Tom, his heart hammering within his chest. He was bathed in sweat and his skin was hot to the touch, as if he had been standing for a long time under a hot desert sun, though he knew he had no fever.

Dark matter. It was dark matter inside him that was making him see Coyote. He marveled at the wonders of the human brain and soul, because even when distorted by dark matter, they were giving him an important message.

Dark matter was inside the sand man that Coyote had created. The attempt to remove it had destroyed the sand man.

Something very bad was about to happen.

Chakotay rose and silently went to the small table at the far end of the hut. He poured water into a bowl and splashed his face, trying to make sense of the dream. It was too logical, in its strange, illogical way, to be simply a dream. He poured some more water from the pitcher into a cup, took a few sips, then went to the window and opened the crude shutters.

It was the deep heart of the night, the quietest hour. Even the night things that called and whistled to one another from the depths of the rain forest seemed hushed. The thick, moist air had settled to the ground as a ghostly fog. This planet had moons very similar to Earth's single luminous orb, and their cool, milky radiance bathed the plants and tinged the slow-moving fog with silver.

Coyote was the Trickster. He loved to joke and play pranks, some more dangerous than others. Some legends said that he created man as a joke or an experiment. Was the dark sand the dark matter, or merely the darkness that dwelt in every human heart, even the brightest and kindest?

But Tialin had cleansed them of the dark matter, had extracted it and placed it into that glowing purple sphere. He and Tom at least were—

But this place wasn't. These people weren't. And who knew whether he and Tom had been reinfected since their arrival. He knew, in a way the Culilann could not, how very different he and Tom were from them. Not just in their embracing of science and technology, but also in their very cells. The Doctor had said something about Khala's DNA sequencing being almost backward from that of humans. Did that apply to everything? Did it apply to the birds he could hear? Was their DNA a complete inversion of that of a parrot or a macaw? The plants, what about them?

And were they all infected with dark matter?

Chakotay made a decision without even realizing that he had been in debate with himself. Kind as the Culilann were, and much as he had grown to like them, he and Tom needed to leave. They had to contact the Alilann, Khala's caste, and speak with them about the potential dangers they faced. Only advanced technology could even recognize the dark matter present in their bodies; only advanced technology had a hope of extracting it. Prayers, meditation, chants, and rituals certainly had their roles in nurturing the soul, but science had to step in now.

Besides, contacting the Alilann was the only way he and Tom could possibly contact *Voyager* and return home.

And yet, this place felt like home now. It had been several days since their official welcoming ceremony, and he and Tom had been put to work as constructive citizens of Sumar-ka. It had been good, simple work, physical labor in the warmth of the suns that left muscles pleasantly aching at day's end. Massages were given as a matter of course to all those who had worked hard—soothing, calming massages with rich oils to moisturize the skin and strong hands, male or female, to unkink knots in the muscles. The food was strengthening but light, and Chakotay felt physically better than he had in a long time. Real, pure food, prepared simply and with care, hard work, sound rest, friendly companions. It was a world away from the intellectual puzzles, recirculated air, and replicated food that comprised life on a starship.

Even as he thought about his time here, Chakotay realized that it was over. They would leave in the morning. He was certain the villagers would protest, but they were not barbarians. They would not prevent him and Tom from leaving if they really wanted to.

Sighing, Chakotay finished the glass of water and returned to his cot. He turned from the window and closed it, and in so doing, missed the slight movement at the edge of the jungle.

Matroci couldn't sleep. He was edgy and nervous, and couldn't imagine why. Chakotay and Paris had accepted their initiation as citizens of Sumar-ka, and they were proving themselves stalwart members of the community. He liked them, different as they were, and their presence here merely reinforced the words of the Crafters, who told the Culilann to welcome Strangers.

And yet, something was nagging at him. Something was not right. He wanted to sleep, but he heaved a sigh, rose, and donned his formal robes. A consultation was needed.

He opened the shutters and went about preparing the Sacred Plant. Lighting it from the small bed of coals he kept burning in a clay jar, he fanned the flames with his hand to increase the smoke.

Matroci coughed. As always.

He forced himself to inhale as much as he could and opened his mind to the will of the Crafters.

Something was not right. The sounds of the jungle ought to be louder. Now, even the night beasts were still. There were no more birdcalls.

Without knowing why, Matroci tasted fear. Why were the beasts of the forest so quiet? He knew he needed to finish the meditation, but he couldn't help himself. He got to his feet and padded to the window. He gulped in the fresh, cool night air and looked around. He had no idea what he expected to see. The larger predators such as the *iislak* disliked the bustle of the village and seldom approached, save in lean times. Still, his gaze searched. Finally, Matroci sighed and turned around to complete the meditation.

The woman stood before him. The moons' light spilled in through the opened window, but did nothing to soften the ice in her eyes and the hardness of her face, of her strange clothing. She was of his kind, but as different from him as she could possibly be. And even as his mind made the identification, as his lips moved to form the word "Alilann," she lifted something, pressed it to his chest, and squeezed.

"Use the chamber pot, Paris," Tom muttered to himself as he stepped carefully on the moist earth. "If you have to go out, take a lamp, Paris. You could get lost out there at night, Paris. Damn, I hate it when he's right."

Used to all the comforts provided by *Voyager,* Paris found that using the small stoneware pots to relieve himself at night was a thoroughly alien concept. It made him uncomfortable, especially with Chakotay in the same small hut. It was one thing when he had been so desperately sick. He didn't care who saw him do what then. But now, modesty had returned along with health, and when nature called in the middle of the night, Paris felt more comfortable going outside to perform the necessary bodily functions.

Chakotay had been right. He should have just used the pot, should have taken a lamp. He had done neither, and now he was lost.

"Ah, come on, Tom," he said, simply to hear the reassuring sound of his own voice in the still darkness. "The moons are nice and bright, and you can't have walked more than a few meters from the encampment."

But the moons' light, bright as it was, stopped when it hit the upper canopy of the thick rain forest.

It didn't filter down here, where moist leaves sucked at his booted feet and every twining vine and branch looked like every other one.

A low, soft sound made him stop dead. His heart began to thud in his chest. He listened, straining, wondering if he could hear anything over the *boom-boom* of his own alarmed heart.

Yes, there it was again. A soft crooning sound. Paris closed his eyes briefly, trying to calm himself. It didn't work. Matroci and Soliss had spoken with him and Chakotay about the dangers of the jungle that began almost at their very door. There weren't many—very few poisonous creatures, only one or two species of large predators who were shy of humanoids and who seldom came near the edge of the rain forest. But there was one they did warn the new members of Sumar-ka about, and that was the *iislak*. It was large and furry and, from the description Soliss had provided, resembled a cross between a pig and a cat. It was carnivorous, and notoriously silent.

"We see its prints," Matroci had said, "and its dung, but very seldom the beast itself. Sometimes there is a warning, a faint noise as of a woman singing a babe to sleep. If you hear that sound, consider yourselves blessed by the Crafters and leap for the nearest tree."

Tom remembered that advice, and immediately looked up. A nice, thick branch dangled invitingly overhead. He sprang upward, ignoring the pain of his broken bones and, wrapping his good arm about its thick, welcome bulk, he kicked his legs up. Grunting, he squirmed, hoisting himself up onto the branch. It was moist with the evening dew and twice he nearly lost his grip. Once he was secure, he did not gloat in his victory. He looked for the next highest branch.

Another sound split the silence, a kind of bleating noise. It was similar to the first sound, but with a frantic, higher edge to it. Once Paris had secured the next branch, he risked looking down.

It was hard to see at first. The moonlight and darkness conspired to camouflage the creature almost perfectly. Then it moved, and it was as if a shadow had come to life, a shadow with large, lambent eyes that fixed on Paris.

It opened its mouth, emitting that bleating noise. "No," Paris whispered. Oh, no. It was a baby *iislak,* separated from its mother, and it was right at the base of his tree.

It did look like a cross between a pig and a cat. Its body was small, the fur appearing baby-soft. Large paws adorned comparatively short legs. A stump of a tail twitched. It was kind of cute, in an ungainly, ugly sort of way. It opened its mouth, situated at the end of a lumpy snout, and again called for its mother.

The crooning sound came again, closer this time. Paris gulped and decided that the next set of branches, higher up, would provide a much better seat from which to view the no-doubt touching reunion.

He was just reaching up when the crooning sound turned into an ear-splitting screech and the tree shook violently. Paris lost his footing and grabbed for a branch with both hands. Again came the awful noise, and again the tree shook. Paris clung on desperately, finally managing to get one knee hooked over the branch. His head dangled down and he couldn't help but look upward at the forest floor.

It was enormous. Big as a horse—bigger—and mad as hell. There was nothing ungainly about Mama *iislak*. She was all knotted muscle and sleek, lean elegance. Even her elongated, porcine muzzle was dangerous-looking, drawn back from teeth that were about as long as Paris's hand. She snarled again and leaped upward, digging her claws into the trunk.

Can it climb? They had told him to seek the shelter of a tree, and he had done so. Had they underestimated Mama's instinct to protect Junior?

But even as he stared, horrified, Paris saw that the long, powerful claws could not support the creature's mammoth weight. Great furrows were etched in the trunk as Mama slid slowly back down to the earth.

Junior cried again, and Mama turned to nuzzle her offspring. It cooed and rubbed its little face against her large, furry, ugly one. A pink tongue, longer than Tom's arm, crept out as Mama licked her baby.

The branch crackled under Paris's weight. Adrenaline shot through him and sweat covered his skin as the branch sank slightly lower.

Mama's head whipped up and she fixed Paris with those enormous eyes. She crooned again, then, nudging Junior along, departed.

For an agonizing length of time, Paris simply hung there. The branch continued to hold, but for how long? And were Mama and Junior really gone, or just waiting? How intelligent were the *iislak,* after all? Idiot that he was, he'd never bothered to ask. He breathed shallowly, not daring to move.

His neck cramped. He took a deep breath and slowly climbed back up to a seated position, edging closer to the wet trunk. Again the branch creaked under him, and Paris threw his arms around the solidity of the tree's trunk.

He thought he'd just stay there awhile, to make certain that the danger had passed. Dawn wasn't that far off, anyway.

Dawn was, as it turned out, several hours away. When the sky finally began to lighten, Paris deemed it safe enough to climb down. His body, stiff from fear and its cramped position, protested as he descended. He hadn't thought he was all that far off the ground when Mama and Junior were down at the base of the tree, but now he saw he was several yards away from the solidity of the earth, closer to the canopy than the ground. Now that one of the suns was beginning to dispel the darkness, he could even glimpse the thatched roofs of the village huts. In the dark, they had looked like just so much foliage.

He made his way down carefully, slipping once or twice, and felt gratitude sweep through him. He almost laughed aloud as his feet finally touched that soggy, wonderful soil.

When he emerged from the rain forest, he found the village in an uproar. People were crying, others were running with grim looks on their faces. Paris swore under his breath and began to run himself.

Everyone stopped when they saw him approach. Paris's pace faltered. He spotted Soliss, who was staring at him with an unreadable expression.

"Soliss, what's happened?"

"You are still here," said Soliss.

"Of course I am," Paris replied. The villagers were starting to move away from him, slowly, as if he were dangerous. "Look, what's going on?"

"Where were you?" It was Winnif, and the challenge was unexpected. Her eyes were swollen from crying.

"Last night I had to—you know. I went to the edge of the forest and I got lost. I somehow got between an *iislak* and her baby and she treed me for the rest of the night. I can take you to the tree, if you'd like. The claw marks are this long. And why are you demanding to know where I was, anyway? What the hell has happened?"

Grimly, Soliss answered him, and Tom wished he hadn't.

"Chakotay is gone and Matroci is dead."

CHAPTER

15

TORRES COULDN'T REMEMBER EVER HAVING SLEPT SO deeply. It seemed as though she had just lain down when the computer woke her at 0600. Her whole body ached as she sat up and stretched. A slight pang went through her as her gaze fell on the empty half of the bed.

Tom. Oh, how she missed him. Missed his wisecracks, his last-minute, frantic, but usually successful attempts at romancing her, the rough-but-sweet physical encounters. More than anything, she missed waking up beside him, seeing his face relaxed in sleep and wreathed in innocence, looking more like a boy's than a man's.

If only they knew what had happened to him.

Most of the time, B'Elanna had mentally integrated Khala as a member of the crew. But now and then, with no warning, she would stop and regard the blue woman with fresh eyes. She was an alien, with a strangeness to her that they had never encountered before, and she was here, and Tom was gone.

And Chakotay. Once an object of misplaced romantic attraction, he was now the dearest friend B'Elanna had in the world. Captain Janeway inspired fierce loyalty and absolute trust, but Chakotay had an ease about him that relaxed the crew in stressful times. Everyone was suffering because of his absence.

"Dammit," she said angrily. She rose and went to the shower. To distract herself from missing Tom and Chakotay—a fruitless exercise that did nothing but cause her heart to contract and distract her from the true business at hand—she turned her attention to the puzzle they'd been working on last night.

That Damned Ball could extract dark matter from transported objects. It could extract it from any plant or any inanimate material placed within the sphere of radiation it created when supplied with sufficient energy. But the radiation would not extract dark matter from humans.

Sufficient energy were the two key words. Torres stepped out of the shower and began to dress. The transporter could provide only a certain amount of energy, and they'd utilized it to the fullest yesterday.

When it occurred to her, Torres literally groaned. It was so obvious, why hadn't she seen it before? Why hadn't anyone seen it before?

She struggled into her uniform, pulled on her boots, carelessly ran a comb through her wild locks, and almost ran to engineering.

"The warp core," she said as she entered. Everyone turned to stare at her. Seven was there, as usual, and Khala and Telek were just coming in.

"What about the warp core?" asked Khala. Her eyes widened. "The warp bubble—it is holding stable, isn't it?"

"Yes, yes," said Torres impatiently. "For the energy. To boost the circumference of the radiation sphere around That Damned Ball. We need to use the warp core."

Torres ordered strong coffee, as close an approximation to fresh-brewed as Neelix could make, sent down from the mess hall. She was both annoyed and gladdened to see that Neelix had also sent down some delicious-looking pastries, conveniently cut into bite-sized pieces for a quick gulp now and then.

"Are these—" began Khala, then she stopped herself. "No, I won't ask. It doesn't really matter whether they're replicated or not, and if I don't ask, I won't be able to tell." With an incongruously grim expression, she picked up a piece of pastry and ate it.

Torres bit back an angry retort. She had, frankly, had it up to here with Khala's reluctance to eat food if it wasn't replicated. Food was food, and if it tasted good and it nourished you, who the hell cared if it came out of the dirt or a replicator? But it was clear that Khala was trying. Which was good, because the next time the alien woman complained about *Voy-*

ager's fresh food, Torres wasn't sure if she could resist shoving it in Khala's face.

They ate and drank and talked excitedly with their mouths full. They ran some simulations, and it looked as if it could work. There was only one slight problem.

"We're going to have to take the warp core offline," Torres stated in a staff meeting a few hours later. "And probably the shields will have to be down as well."

Janeway raised an eyebrow. "I see," she said.

"Everything seems to point toward a direct proportional increase," said Telek. "If we were to attempt to cleanse a ship, for instance, we would require less power than if we were attempting to cleanse a whole planet."

"I do not like the idea of our vessel being so vulnerable," said Tuvok.

"None of us does," said Janeway. "But it sounds like that's a risk we're going to have to take in order to completely accomplish our goal. Give it to me in detail, B'Elanna."

Torres did. Once the warp core was off-line, all its energy could be harnessed in the purple sphere. The radiation would increase proportionally. The more energy, the larger the sphere. In theory, with enough energy, the sphere could expand thousands of kilometers, easily large enough to embrace an entire moon or planet. The radiation would purge the planet's plants, inanimate objects, and lesser life forms of dark matter; they would have to transport the rest. It would be time-consuming, risky to the ship, and exhausting—but it was doable.

"We'll need to run some tests," finished Torres, "and engineering is continuing to transport the Kwaisi."

"Ulaahn has been asking me about his vessels and his homeworld," said Janeway. "I've been stalling until now. The holodeck is of course at your disposal for any simulations you need to run. The minute you think you've got something, let me know. We can try our first test on Ulaahn's ship."

As she rose, anxious to begin the holodeck simulations, B'Elanna's gaze fell on Harry. He had never been particularly good at hiding his emotions, and he looked like a kicked puppy right now. Khala was seated as far away from him as she could get and still be in the room, and her attempt at casualness around Harry only revealed that whatever was going on, or not going on, between them was anything but casual.

Torres swallowed her impatience and lingered long enough to speak to Harry. "What's up, Starfleet? You look pretty—" Torres bit her lip. She had been about to say "blue," but that was clearly not a good color to remind Harry of right now.

"I don't want to talk about it." Kimspeak for *something really bad is going on and I'm in a lot of pain.*

"Lunch at twelve hundred," said Torres. "On me."

"I'd rather not."

"That's an order, Ensign. I outrank you, remember?" She tried to soften it, make it teasing, but Harry was too miserable for any jest to reach. For the millionth time, she wished Tom were here, and not just for her own selfish pleasure. Tom could get a smile out of Harry when no one else could. Kim was not smiling as he nodded and pushed past her.

Janeway was beginning to think she liked Ulaahn better with dark matter inside him.

He had been suicidal and despondent, but there had been a sorrow about him and a sluggishness that Janeway had been able to use to both their advantages. Now, freed of the influence of dark matter on his mind and body, Ulaahn was brash, all quick moves and loud demands. As he stormed onto her bridge, head held high, Janeway braced herself.

"Captain Janeway," said Ulaahn, "You must hasten this process. A full fifth of my crew are still infected with dark matter. And my ships! *When* are you going to purge my ships? There is an entire system affected with this dreadful plague, and we have to reach them and help them!"

"Commander Ulaahn," replied Janeway in as soft and mild a voice as she was capable of at that moment, "We are working as fast as we can within safety parameters. Chief Engineer Torres—"

"Is frustratingly slow and inefficient!" railed Ulaahn. "And what kind of safety parameters are we talking about? Are you telling me you don't know what you're doing?"

"I'm telling you," said Janeway, stretching her lips into a grimace of a smile, "that we are working with alien technology that is almost as new to us as it is to you. The last thing we want is casualties from rushing the process."

"Dead is dead, Captain," said Ulaahn, stepping in

close and trying to use his height to appear more imposing. "I doubt that a corpse cares if it dies because of an error or because the dark matter has ravaged its brain!"

"Perhaps not." Oh, her voice was so calm. "But the living being who is next in line might care a great deal. What you are failing to realize, Commander, is that my ship, too, is infected; some of my crew still are. We are giving your people priority because the infection is more severe. It is in all of our interests to find the fastest, safest way to rid everything we can of the dark matter. Raising your voice and attempting crude bullying tactics will not make this work go any faster."

His eyes blazed, but she continued. She lifted her chin and narrowed her blue eyes. "You are a guest aboard my ship. Your people are guests. We are doing everything we can, as quickly as we can, to help you and your people survive. I suggest you behave accordingly."

She heard the soft movement behind her as Tuvok moved a few feet away from his station. It was not an overtly menacing move, just a subtle reminder of Tuvok's position as chief of security. Ulaahn glanced from one to the other and growled low in his throat. He threw himself down into Chakotay's chair and sat, sullen and silent.

It was not exactly what Janeway had wanted, but it would do.

"Engineering to Janeway."

"Go ahead, Torres." It was a welcome and timely interruption.

"The warp core is now off-line. We're ready to proceed with the test on your order."

Janeway glanced over at her Kwaisi counterpart. "Commander? May we begin the test?"

He frowned. "Of course, test your unknown device out on my vessel, not your own."

"Well," said Janeway, as if she were talking to a child, "actually, both vessels will be affected. The radiation sphere will have to be larger than *Voyager* if it's to be large enough to engulf your vessel."

"Yes, yes, I understand, go ahead."

Janeway smothered a smile. "You may proceed, Lieutenant." Her voice was calm, but inside she was tense. What if something went wrong? Not only with Ulaahn's ship, but with their own? Tuvok had been right. Bringing the warp core off-line and having to lower their shields made them incredibly vulnerable. But there seemed to be no other choice.

The shields were already down; she did not have to issue the order. The bridge was utterly silent as everyone stared at the screen. In the center was a vacant vessel, oblong and pale cream-gray. If all went well, it would look identical after this test, except it would be infinitely safer for living things to inhabit. And they would be that much closer to accomplishing a Herculean task.

"On your order, Captain," said Torres.

"Do it," said Janeway.

Torres swallowed, and pressed the control.

The horrible sound screeched forth and Torres

closed her eyes against the accompanying bright-
ness. "Seven, report."

Seven had to shout to be heard over the noise. "The
radiation sphere is increasing by six percent . . . thirty-
six . . . one thousand two hundred ninety-six . . . it is
now engulfing the entire ship. The dark matter within
the affected area has been contained within the orb."

"So far, so good," yelled Torres.

"The sphere is expanding. It has crossed the distance to the Kwaisi vessel. It is presently engulfing
the vessel."

How Torres wished she could see it, but even the
experimental goggles the Doctor had constructed
didn't help. She'd just have to experience it vicari-
ously through Seven. Her heart was racing, and she
realized her palms were wet.

Please let this work.

The light began to fade, and the awful sound
ceased. Torres blinked.

"Did it work?" asked Khala anxiously.

Seven did not reply at once. "The amount of dark
matter contained within the warp-core bubble has increased eighteen point seven percent. There is no trace
of dark matter within the targeted Kwaisi vessel." She
looked up, fixed Khala with her cool gaze, and said,
"The attempt appears to have been successful."

There were some very unprofessional sounds of
whooping from engineering, and Torres thought
even Seven seemed to smile a little.

Harry Kim captured a piece of broccoli with his
chopsticks. "So then the captain says, 'Well, Com-

mander, it seems as though within a few hours we'll have your crew and vessels back in perfect working order.' And Ulaahn says, 'Well, Captain, it's about time.' "

"What a jerk," said Torres, with feeling. "We're working around the clock here to help him out and that's the best he can do?"

"He's been following the captain around ever since we beamed him over, yelling at her to hurry up, make everything all right again. Frankly, I'm going to be delighted when we see the last of the Kwaisi."

Torres took a big bite of her corned-beef sandwich and wiped her mouth. "I don't know. Some of them have been very cooperative and polite. It may just be Ulaahn. Can't make snap judgments about a whole species based on a single individual, Harry. You know that."

Which was apparently the wrong thing to say. Harry froze in mid-chew. He deliberately swallowed the bite, folded his napkin, and rose. He was only halfway through his meal.

Torres mentally kicked herself. She reached out and gently closed her hand around his wrist. "Neelix worked hard on making that Szechwan *yruss*-and-broccoli for you, Harry. Go ahead and finish it."

"I've lost my appetite."

"Then I'll have some," she said casually, leaning over the table to spear up a slice of surprisingly tasty *yruss*. She knew this bothered Harry and was pleased when he frowned and said, "Hey, cut it out."

Smiling, she popped the bite in her mouth and chewed. "Mmm. I may have to have some of that next time he makes it. So come on, Harry, what's wrong? I know you're interested in Khala, and while I admit she's got some strange food preferences, she seems nice enough. She certainly seems interested in *you.*"

"*Seems* is the operative word," said Harry, pitching his voice soft. He looked around to make sure there was no one close enough to overhear. "I just don't get this whole caste system her people have. It seems so odd, so arbitrary."

"Come on, Starfleet, we've encountered odder customs before. This whole journey has been an exercise in cultural appreciation. Remember the Karakish? The ones with the—"

"Okay, okay," he said, laughing a little now. His cheeks were red. Torres grinned and picked up her sandwich. "If she were just a guest on the ship, it'd be one thing. But we don't know how long she's going to be here, B'Elanna. And she's more than just another visitor to the ship. I really care about her. And she—she can't understand me at all."

Torres thought about how Khala brightened every time Harry dropped by engineering. She thought about the conversation she'd accidentally overheard, when Khala had shyly asked Seven about appropriate dress for her dinner with Harry. She thought about how often poor Kim had gotten his heart broken and how nice it would be to see him with someone who might actually be worthy of him.

"What doesn't she understand?" she asked, very gently.

Harry glanced down at his hands for a moment,

then up at Torres. "My music. She didn't even know what it was when I talked about it."

"Did you play for her?"

Miserably, he nodded. "I wish I hadn't. B'Elanna, you wouldn't believe it. She got this look on her face like she was going to be sick. And that's what she called it. Sick. Wrong. And then she just walked out."

Torres was horrified. "Harry, I'm so sorry. Seems like we have two alien jerks on this vessel."

He shook his dark head. "No, no, she wasn't trying to be mean. She was crying when she left. But I can't avoid her. She's here for who knows how long. And she thinks my favorite thing in the world to do is sick." He managed a wan smile. "Tom was right. I sure can pick them, can't I? Thanks for lunch, B'Elanna, and . . . for talking with me. Sorry I couldn't enjoy it more."

This time, she didn't try to stop him.

INTERLUDE

THIS TIME IT WAS NOT A PLANET, BUT A SHIP THAT CALLED to the Entity. And this time, the Entity knew it knew those who crewed it.

Kazon.

They had once been slaves until they had over-thrown their cruel masters, the Trabe. They had scattered the Trabe throughout the quadrant, but centuries of squabbling among themselves had prevented any chance of unification. They were small, angry sects, grabbing territory here and there, stealing technology, crushing the spirits of their females and drumming war and anger into the skulls of their young sons at too tender an age.

Son. Yes, that was why it was here. A child was

dying from the ravages of the dark matter in its system. And though the Entity knew that there was no reason for it to love the Kazon, it felt pity for an innocent child.

It engulfed the ship, gently, so as not to draw attention to its presence. Now it was on the bridge of the vessel, and a violent argument was taking place.

"You are growing soft, Maje!" one was crying. "Once, you had Voyager within your grasp. How we permitted you to remain maje of the Kazon-Nistrim, I do not know."

Names the Entity knew: Voyager, Nistrim. And it knew that the haggard-looking maje who slumped in the command chair was called Culluh.

"You lost the burning in your heart when you lost Seska," the underling continued. "For a woman, Culluh! A female and her suckling babe!"

The maje seemed to stir, and a hint of anger sparkled in his eyes. "You were told never to mention her name. And as for our son—"

"Seska!" said the underling in a singsong voice. "Seska, Seska, dead, dead, dead! Just like her brat will be in—"

Culluh roared to life. He screamed his rage, leaped up from the chair, and flung himself at the insubordinate underling. The Entity recoiled from the fury, and for an instant wondered why there was no trace of dark matter, and why it did not sense the awful feeling of malevolence in Maje Culluh.

Then it understood. The emotions pouring off Culluh were grief and . . . love. He had loved Seska, loved her strength of will and her cunning, even when she played him for a fool. The soft flow of hair, the ridge of hard bone on the brow—all of these things were committed to Culluh's mind forever, superceding his previous passion, power. And the son—he loved this boy. And the boy was dying from the dark matter.

With a thought, the Entity was in the maje's private room. A small shape huddled on the bed. As the Entity watched, he moaned and writhed. It could see parts of him appearing and disappearing, and ached with compassion.

It wanted to assume a form the boy would know and trust, but did not know how to do so. Perhaps later it would. It would apply itself to learning how. But for now, it simply settled on the boy like a soft draping of mist, and pulled all the wrong things into itself.

The boy—half Cardassian, half Kazon, all innocence at this tender age—sighed. He relaxed. His body was stable and whole again, and his brain had not been damaged by the attack of the wrong things.

One more thing to do here.

It returned again to the bridge. The maje had triumphed for the moment. Gently the Entity passed through the maje and planted a soft suggestion in his brain: Go to your son.

Culluh blinked, but the suggestion was too strong. He fairly raced through the ship, and the Entity could read his thoughts. He was certain his child was dying—his child, his only link to the treacherous, sensuous woman he had so adored.

The boy was sitting up in bed. "I had an awful

dream, Father," he said. "I dreamed my legs were—"

But Culluh, heedless of the softness the gesture revealed, had caught the boy up in a tight embrace. He whispered his son's name over and over again, kissing his dark, furrowed brow. The boy hugged back, tightly.

The Entity knew its task was to gather up the wrong things, but it could not resist. It settled itself on father and son, and so gently that it could not be noticed, planted a thought in the father's brain.

This is the way. This is ever the way. Nothing lasting and true can be bought by blood or hatred.

It did not know if the maje would remember this moment, but it knew that, for this brief instant as he held his miraculously cured son, Maje Culluh agreed with the Entity.

CHAPTER
16

THERE HAD BEEN NO SLEEP FOR EITHER JEKRI OR HER second-in-command that night of the attempted assassination. Jekri had called up a list of every person on the *Tektral,* and together she and Verrak had discussed them all: their loyalty, possible areas of blackmail, any incidents that might have seemed to be insignificant but might reveal something quite dark. Jekri had ordered that their doctor bring them stimulants, so that they might not lose their edge. Using stimulants was something she was not fond of doing; the practice had its own price to pay afterward, but right now it was imperative that they remain alert and awake.

Even as they discussed, person by person, the crew of the ship, Jekri wondered if it was not an exercise in futility. Certainly Sharibor would have been regarded as a highly trustworthy individual, and look what she had been. Still, there was precious little else they could do at the moment.

They were deep in conversation over a low-ranking crew member when Jekri's console beeped. They both gasped, startled. For a long moment, Jekri stared at it. It beeped again.

She rose and went to her desk. On the screen there was a message:

Is she dead?

"Sharibor's master," said Verrak, whispering, though there was no one to hear.

"Or my unknown ally," said Jekri. " 'She' could refer to either of us." Messages were almost always verbal and visual in this day and age, but there was a keyboard for instances when the chairman of the Tal Shiar wished to receive and send messages without revealing her identity. Sometimes a sender felt the same way. She had made use of this nonrevealing technology, though under better circumstances. Jekri took a deep breath and typed in an answer:

Yes.

For a long, tense moment, there was no reply. Jekri was ashamed that her hands trembled. She punched a few buttons so that the conversation would be recorded. There might be a chance they could trace the message if the conversation failed to reveal the sender's identity.

That was foolish.

Jekri swore.

You cannot trace me. It is safer that way.

Safer for whom? Jekri tapped in furiously.

For both of us.

"And who is that?" Jekri muttered under her breath. This was the deadliest game she had yet played, conducted on a computer with primitive keys to type in words. It was ironic. What to ask without revealing herself?

So, what is next? she typed.

That is entirely up to you.

A long pause.

Little Dagger.

The person at the other end obviously knew who she was, but Jekri was no more enlightened than before. She searched her mind for questions, but then a beep alerted her that the signal had been terminated. She slammed a fist down on the desk and swore.

"It could have been anyone!" she cried in frustration. "And now whoever it is knows I survived."

"Everyone will know that in the morning," Verrak said logically, "even the one who sent that message. Sharibor was not operating alone, in all likelihood."

Jekri turned to gaze at the corpse on the floor. Verrak was right. And now the word was out. Every bounty hunter in the Empire would be after her now. How many were on this ship alone? Her victory over Sharibor proved that she had not lost her edge, but how many could she evade before simple probabilities won out?

"I know you have a particular fondness for the Empress," said Verrak haltingly. "And a particular dislike for Lhiau. But you must consider all possibilities, Chairman. Could the Empress have sent this?"

Jekri shook her dark head. "It is not her way. I could believe that she would want me dead, but she would execute me in a very public manner. She would wish to shame me before she killed me if she wanted me to die."

"The Praetor? The Proconsul?"

Jekri thought back to the recent conversations she had had with the Praetor. "He tried to warn me on two different occasions," she said, "but that could have been a false face, to lull me into trusting him. After Sharibor—after the assassination attempt, I do not know who to trust anymore."

"I am honored that you trust me," said Verrak softly.

She smiled faintly at him. "We have been alone in this room for hours, Verrak. You have had ample chances to murder your chairman. That you did not take them shows that I may trust you."

She hurt him with the words and she knew it, but they were true. His lack of action, not his apparent love for her, was what she trusted. Love could be faked. She knew—she'd done it herself before. Missing a good chance to kill for money and career advancement could not.

"With this order, I have become a glorious target. I am safe nowhere. Such an extravagant decree speaks of someone who does not respect the secrecy of the Family of the Blade. Any high-ranking Romulan would send out one or two assassins, not this overblown order that would send any greedy would-be killer after the chairman of the Tal Shiar. This is all Lhiau's doing."

"But Lhiau could not issue such a decree without

the overt or at least tacit approval of either the Praetor or the Empress."

Jekri nodded. She had already determined that. He would not have had access to the technology required without clearance. Her mind went back to the tense, unpleasant gathering of several weeks ago. The Empress had been a flighty, twittery girl, not the magnificent ruler she had always been. She had yielded utterly to Lhiau. She had approved the madness of an attack on the Federation without the support of *Voyager*. She had permitted her chairman of the Tal Shiar—*her* chairman, not Lhiau's—to be publicly humiliated.

This was not the behavior of a woman whose mind was her own. Jekri knew that Lhiau could penetrate her mind, could read thoughts. Could he also place them? Was he mentally manipulating the Empress into dancing to the tune he piped?

"What will you do?" Verrak asked.

So, what is next?

That is entirely up to you. Little Dagger.

There was only one thing she could do, one course of action she could pursue. She had to clear her name, or else the rest of her life—which would doubtless be brief, as Jekri had every respect for the skills of the Family of the Blade—would be spent looking over her shoulder.

She alone seemed to recognize the threat Lhiau posed to her people, although as yet she did not know the true nature of that threat. But no one would listen to her now, not while she wore the stigma of *traitor.*

There was only one thing to do. She would clear her name.

It was, as many things are, easier said than done, and before she could even begin to set so complex a plan in motion, Jekri needed to deal with more immediate problems.

Verrak forged a message that requested Sharibor's immediate presence back on Romulus, due to a family emergency. He also beamed the body out into space as disparate particles and erased the transport from the computer's automatic log. Jekri arranged for the Krel family to quietly disappear. She did not issue an order to kill Sharibor's husband and two sons. They would get what information they could first. She knew it was likely that Sharibor's family would die innocent of any wrongdoing. The Family of the Blade fooled nearly everyone, including close family members, but Jekri was not about to let the opportunity slip through her fingers.

Next, she assigned four of her most trustworthy agents to follow the Empress, the Praetor, the Proconsul, and Lhiau. These were considered high-risk assignments, and her agents were compensated accordingly. She had not wanted to employ them yet, as she knew that they would in all likelihood be discovered unless they were very good, very careful and, most important, very lucky, but the death order from Lhiau had forced her hand.

For the next day or two, she behaved normally, though her senses were heightened and she seemed to see assassins in every shadow. There was no further attempt on her life, which, oddly, did nothing to reassure her.

One thing had been worrying her: her conversation with Sharibor about the encrypted message. There had been thirty-five people on duty in that section at that time, and no one had seemed surprised at the conversation Jekri and her chief of encryption had conducted. Had Jekri's unknown ally forced Sharibor's hand by not only alerting Jekri about the message, but making it general knowledge? *Had* Sharibor's team actually been trying to crack the code for several hours? Jekri saw it in her mind's eye—the late assassin, sweat on her brow, pretending to try to crack a code while all the while doing everything she could to prevent its being deciphered. It was a picture that gave her tremendous pleasure to imagine.

One thing she had learned was that, according to Sharibor's team, their chief had not been able to decipher the code. She had gone, apparently unhappily, to report her failure to Jekri that evening.

Jekri had told them to cease their attempts and ordered the message completely wiped from the system. There were a few raised eyebrows at the order, but they complied. She checked a few hours later to make sure her order had been obeyed.

The message was gone, but the mysteries lingered.

Jekri had no family, so she did not have to worry about their being abducted or killed. There was the possibility that Lhiau's spies had traced her activities with the pro-Vulcan group, but if so, why had they not flaunted their knowledge and dragged her forward as a traitor? She would have made it extremely convenient for them to accuse her.

And finally, most perplexing of all: Who was her unknown ally?

The imperial demand came as a shock.

Jekri was in her quarters, three different weapons within easy reach, when the door sounded.

She tensed, as she always did now. The fingers of her right hand closed on the disruptor. "Come," she called.

It was one of her centurions, who saluted briskly. "Honored Chairman!" he barked. "I have a message for you. It is marked for your eyes only."

Jekri tensed, but feigned nonchalance. "Put it on the table," she said, pretending to return to reading a report.

He saluted again—he was obviously one of the new recruits, young and full of a devotion to etiquette—and placed it down. Turning smartly, he left. The door hissed shut behind him.

Jekri licked her lips. She did not want to read this message. It wasn't logical, and no doubt young Tarya would frown in disapproval at her response, but somehow she knew this missive contained bad news.

Steeling herself for the worst, she picked it up and read.

Jekri Kaleh, nominally chairman of the Tal Shiar, is commanded to appear before the Empress tomorrow morning at dawn to answer charges of treason. The Romulan Right of Statement will be observed at this time.

The missive bore the electronic seal of the Empire. That meant the Empress herself had authorized it.

"No," Jekri whispered. "No, Empress, you cannot possibly . . ." Her voice trailed off.

Her worst fear had been realized. Lhiau had managed to convince the Empress and the Praetor of Jekri's guilt. What kind of evidence had he falsified, or had he even needed to do so? Had he not simply stepped into the Empress's lively mind and raped it, twisted it to his own ends?

She ordered Verrak to come to her quarters. When he entered, she thrust the missive at him. The healthy green bled from his face. His dark eyes met her silver ones over the missive.

"You must act quickly," he said.

She shook her head. "There is no time. And I am still chairman of the Tal Shiar, and a loyal Romulan. No, Verrak. I must go before the Empress. Perhaps she will listen to me."

The words sounded hollow in her own ears, and she saw their emptiness reflected on Verrak's stricken face.

It was not everyone, Jekri mused wryly, who had the opportunity to choose how they would face their own death. She wore her most formal uniform and placed every commendation she had ever been awarded on her left breast. No cosmetics for her. This was life-and-death business, regardless of the formality of the situation. Let them see the wrinkles just starting to appear around silver eyes that saw everything; let them observe the pallor and circles under those eyes, mute testimony to sleepless nights spent in service to the Empire.

Verrak had spent half the night pleading with her to plan an escape if things did not turn out well. Jekri had not listened. Such things were for cowards. She had been ordered to appear before the Senate and its Proconsul, the Praetor, and the Empress in her office as chairman of the Tal Shiar. She would not disgrace the position she had done so much to earn.

So it was that when they came for her, three strange, inscrutable centurions whose names she never learned, she stood ready and awaiting them. They roughly seized her arms. With an ease that clearly surprised them, she broke their grip.

"There is no need for such actions," she said mildly. "I will not resist." She had meditated for three hours before they were due to come for her, and she felt calm and refreshed. She even felt a little hopeful. Perhaps her words would finally do some good.

The centurions ignored her, and grabbed her again. She resigned herself to their rough handling.

No one, not even Verrak, came to see her off.

It was as familiar as her own quarters aboard the *Tektral*, this hall down which she now entered as a captive of the Romulan Empire. She marched, head held high and silver eyes gleaming, at the center of a group of centurions. Their booted feet made a martial music as they strode down the smooth stone floor of the Romulan Senate chambers.

They had bound her hands. The ropes chafed, and

green blood was starting to appear on the rough surface.

How often had she herself led such a brigade,
marching forward with a traitor to the Empire bound
behind her? But this time, it was a role reversal that
chilled her to her very core, even as she knew that
there had been no honorable alternative to this moment.

Tramp. Tramp. Tramp. Tramp.

She saw, as if for the first time, the rainbow hues
of the banners of every noble house of the Empire.
The colors were almost painfully bright. The chill
that permeated this room at all times felt to her particularly cold. Her senses were heightened, but from
fear or from weeks of attentive meditation, or possibly both, Jekri could not tell.

And at the far end of the endless-seeming walk,
the Empress sat on a throne that had not been
moved from this site for centuries. She wore her favorite color, red, today, Jekri noticed with a strange
detachment. Hadn't the Empress worn red the day
that Jekri had come with Lhiau at her side? The day
that had set the stage for this hour, this moment?
Oh, she had been full of arrogance then. She, Jekri
Kaleh, had found Ambassador Lhiau, who had
brought the flawless cloaking device with him, who
had corrupted the Empress's mind, who had been
directly responsible for Jekri's presence here as a
prisoner instead of one of the highest ranking Romulans in the Empire.

On the Empress's right stood Lhiau. He was clad
in soft robes of pastel colors that made his fair fea-

tures and golden hair look striking. He did not bother to conceal his pleasure at seeing his rival brought so low. To the Empress's left, in Jekri's old position, stood the Praetor. His expression was unreadable.

Were you friend or foe, those times when you warned me, Praetor? Jekri wondered. *Either way, you had best be careful. Lhiau stands in your old place, on the Empress's right. You stand where I ought to. If I can fall, old friend, then so can you.*

Anger washed over her, and she tasted bitterness. If she could undo that day, she would, but such wishes were futile. She had made the choices that had brought her here. And looking back over them, Jekri realized that she could not have done anything else.

The long walk ended at last. Jekri stood at the foot of a long stairway, looking up at her Empress. A strong hand on her shoulder slammed her to the floor in a kneeling posture. Her kneecaps hurt from the impact of the unforgiving stone, but she did not so much as grimace.

They all waited for the Empress to speak. Jekri bowed her head, but out of the corner of her eye she could see the senators and the Proconsul, staring like puppets.

"Jekri Kaleh," the Empress said at last, her voice heavy. Surprised, Jekri looked up. There was what appeared to be genuine regret on the Empress's beautiful face. "Little Dagger. I have known you all my life, and trusted you most of it. You cannot know how deeply it pains me to see you here like this."

Hope fluttered in Jekri's heart. If the Empress's

words were true, perhaps there was indeed a chance of reaching her, even though Lhiau hovered over like a predator waiting to strike.

"It pains me to be here," Jekri ventured, "as I have committed no treason, Your Excellency."

It was the wrong thing to say. The Empress's slender brows furrowed and she lifted a hand. Jekri reeled from the unexpected blow of a sword pommel slammed into her temple. For a moment, all went black, then the world swirled back to gray again. She felt a trickle of warm blood down her face, but did not dare lift her bound hands to wipe it away.

This was bad, very bad. She had been through this scene a thousand times, and never had she seen the Empress resort to ordering violence. The prisoner was safely in hand. There was no need to cause pain unless it brought forth information.

"You have committed numerous acts of treason, Little Dagger," spat the Empress. "How dare you lie to me like this?"

Jekri's throat closed up, and she realized with horror that she was close to tears. She could not speak, did not dare speak, until the time had come when by all rights she would be permitted to speak freely without interruption. She held her tongue and listened.

Listened to trumped-up charges of treason read aloud in the Praetor's squeaky voice. He listed contacts with Federation spies and the information she had apparently given them. He spoke of conversations that had never taken place but which, he assured the Senate and Proconsul, had been recorded and would be played at the appropriate time. Jekri wondered if the engineers who had falsified the evidence were still alive, or if they had been dispatched once their usefulness had ended.

There was no arguing against this, and Jekri almost smiled at the irony. Time was when she had someone in her grasp whom she knew to be a traitor, but could not prove it. Once, she had been where the Praetor was, speaking charges she knew were false to ensure an ultimate justice.

Except this time, it was all lies. The only treason she had committed was a mistrust of an imperial ally, one who had pierced her thoughts and—

She blinked, and her silver eyes flickered back to Lhiau. He was frowning now, staring right at her. A tiny flame of triumph sprang to life inside Jekri. He could not read her thoughts! Surely at this moment, his moment of victory, he would be inside her head gloating. But she could feel nothing, hear nothing. The Vulcan disciplines had worked. She returned his gaze, and smiled slowly. This, at least, she had achieved.

Lhiau broke eye contact and gazed at someone who was coming up behind Jekri. Now, he relaxed and smiled, quirking an eyebrow as he regarded Jekri. She did not have to read his mind to know that whoever was approaching the imperial dais would seal Jekri's fate.

Jekri tried to crane her neck; the movement hurt, but not as much as seeing who her final betrayer was.

Verrak.

He bowed before his Empress and Praetor, and stood stiffly at attention. He did not look at Jekri at all.

"I, Verrak Kamaral, Subcommander of the Imperial vessel the *Tektral,* come before my Empress, my Praetor, my Proconsul and the Imperial Senate with more evidence to be used against Jekri Kaleh." They had stopped even pretending that her title was of any value. "I know that she is a murderer, a liar, and a traitor, and I will testify to anything the court demands. I have kept extensive notes regarding her activities and when possible have recorded them."

The blow to her temple was a love pat compared to the pain that surged through Jekri at these words. Verrak. She had thought he loved her, had deemed him the single person she could trust. And he seemed to be taking a sort of gleeful pleasure in betraying her to the hated Lhiau. All their conversations were now being spoken; all their plans laid bare, naked to the scrutiny of those who had made up their minds about her before she ever set foot inside these halls.

And the final blow: "She has been fraternizing with Vulcan sympathizers." He turned and looked at her, his eyes cold. "I had her followed. It is unlikely you will be able to extract information forcibly from her through regular methods because of the *disciplines"*—he sneered the word as if it were something filthy—"she has mastered sitting at the feet of pacifists."

"There is one final thing before we pronounce your sentence," said the Empress. "You have the Right of Statement. Do you choose to accept it or waive it?"

"I accept," she said, her voice sounding thin and hesitant. The centurions helped her to her feet as the recording device was brought to her. The impassive master of the device tapped on the controls, then stood back, waiting.

Now that the time had come, Jekri was at a loss for words. Verrak's betrayal had taken the last traces of fire, of hope, out of her. She was exhausted, wrung out like a limp rag, and her tongue felt thick and sluggish in her mouth.

She dragged her gaze up to the dais and regarded Lhiau. He was smirking. That gave her the energy she needed.

"I stand before you as a condemned prisoner," she began. She knew the ritual opening by heart, but had never thought she herself would be speaking these words. "But prisoner or no, I am a Romulan, and to that end I record my final statement. My crime is treason, but, my friends, I am no traitor. I am as loyal a servant to the highest goals of the Romulan Empire as can be found on this planet or any other. Everything I have done, and everything I have thought, and everything for which I have striven has been to further those goals.

"There stands before you one who does not have the interests of the Empire in his heart. His name is Lhiau of the Shepherds, who has wormed his way into the highest ranks and spreads corruption and lies wherever he touches."

There were murmurs, but no one interrupted her. She could speak whatever she liked now. They would not stop her, no matter what she said.

"He comes, bearing a tantalizing prize—quadrant domination. This is achieved solely by trusting him and his technology, technology that I believe with all my heart to be directly responsible for the destruction of our thirteen warbirds and some of the finest warriors the Empire has ever birthed. What do we know about this technology? Why did we choose to implement it so freely? My friends, fellow Romulans, I believe we were duped. Duped by Lhiau.

"He asks us to defeat his enemies. Has he even named them? He takes our Empress, our beautiful, proud, strong Empress whom I honor above all females as what a Romulan should be, and makes her a *fvai* to sit at his feet and wag her tail at his words!"

The outbursts were loud and angry this time, and the Empress rose from her chair. Jekri continued frantically.

"Empress, I have always served you and this Empire with my whole being. I know that I am nothing without the Empire. Why do you throw it away? I have felt Lhiau's presence in my mind like a rapist. He can read thoughts, can influence them. You are under his influence even now, and you are too blind to see!" She whirled, facing the senators. "All of you are! We will pay for your blindness, your heedlessness, your self-serving rejection of your duty. We will pay terribly. I, fortunately, will be long dead by the time Lhiau topples the Empire and places the crown of Emperor on his pretty golden head. And for that I am glad, I am glad. But you will have to see, and know, and remember this moment when I, Jekri Kaleh, once chairman of the Tal Shiar, stood before you and warned you of the dire consequences of your misplaced ambition.

"Beware of Lhiau and his conniving ways. Beware those who would lie and falsify evidence. If it can happen to me, it can happen to you, from the lowliest peasant to the Praetor himself. Beware, oh my people. Beware, and remember the words of the Little Dagger before she died."

She sagged, utterly drained by the passion that had blazed through her. She barely felt rough hands seize her and drag her off. She knew where she was going—to a cell to await her painful execution. They might try torture, they might not. At this moment, she was too drained to care.

But she was not too drained to care when she passed Verrak, and he gazed at her with contempt before looking away.

CHAPTER

17

CHAKOTAY OPENED HIS EYES AND WONDERED IF HE
was still dreaming. He saw not the thatched roof of
the hut nor the cool hues of *Voyager*'s bulkhead, but
blue skies and bright sunlight filtered through cool
green leaves. And that scene was swaying from side
to side.

"You're awake. Good," came a voice. "You were
starting to get pretty heavy."

Chakotay realized he was being carried on a litter,
which was now being set down. He got to his feet,
memories coming back to him. He had been asleep,
having another one of his confusing and vexing
dreams about the mischievous Coyote, when he had
woken to the sight of a young man pointing a

weapon at him. There had not even been time to inhale for a breath to shout.

"Who are you?" he demanded. "Why have you abducted me?"

The young man who had aimed the weapon at him stepped forward. "It's not an abduction, Chakotay. It's a liberation. I am Shamraa Ezbai Remilkansuur, leader of this recovery expedition. We are the Alilann. We've gone to a great deal of trouble to get you."

The Alilann. The very people Chakotay had wanted to leave the Culilann to see. "You have a very odd welcoming committee," he said.

Ezbai smiled a little. He was wet, dirty, and tired-looking. Chakotay got the impression that he was not used to these so-called recovery expeditions.

"We do not wish to reveal our presence to the Culilann," he said. "This is standard procedure once aliens have been subjected to the Ordeal and integrated into the village. Please accept our apologies. We would have spared you the Ordeal if we could have. But you appeared so suddenly. We never saw a ship, nor intercepted word of a transport in progress. How is it you did this?"

"It's a long story," said Chakotay. "Where's Paris?"

Ezbai's face grew somber. "We were not able to locate him. There were signs that you shared your dwelling with someone, but he was not present."

Chakotay groaned a little. He bet he knew where Tom had gone. Ensign Paris was probably frantic by now, wondering what had happened to Chakotay.

"I'll bet they're organizing search parties to comb

the jungle," he said. "They probably think I wandered away and got lost."

"That's what we want them to think," said a woman, striding forward. Unlike her commander, she looked completely at home here in the dense, hot tangles of the jungle. Her face was young to be as hard as it was. Her eyes were like chips of ice. "They'll start to think they've wasted their time trying to be kind to you, to make you one of them. They'll think twice about bringing any more aliens into their village and subjecting them to the Ordeal."

"Or they may take to killing aliens on sight," retorted Chakotay. He did not like the way this woman spoke. "They may just decide that the Ordeal is an inconvenience."

The woman scowled. "Unlikely. Their gods wouldn't like that." Everyone chuckled a little, apparently at the concept that the Culilann had gods and that gods were anything to be respectful of. Which really bothered Chakotay.

"What is your name?" asked Chakotay.

She straightened and performed what was clearly a salute. "Kilaa Ioni Alimankuur."

"Kilaa Ioni, you have not lived among the Culilann. I have. Their Ordeal is no picnic, but they are essentially a kind and generous people. I would suggest you refrain from insulting something you obviously know nothing about."

Her pale blue brows drew together and she was about to retort, but Ezbai interrupted her. "You are not thinking clearly, Chakotay. You must be experiencing the aftereffects of our stunner. Let us make haste to leave the forbidden parameter and get you to a proper place of rest and nourishment, hmmm?"

Chakotay nodded and gave Ioni a last, angry glance. He would let the matter drop. It was becoming clear to him that each group held strong, negative prejudices about the other, and an argument with a single individual out here in the steamy rain forest was not going to change anyone's mind.

He fell in step beside Ezbai. A thought occurred to him. "You didn't hurt anyone in the village, did you?"

Ezbai looked offended. "Of course not. What do you think we are, primitives like the Culilann? It's they who abandon their children. If it weren't for us, they'd have dozens of infant deaths on their hands."

"What do you mean?"

"Who do you think takes the children?"

A strange relief washed through Chakotay. "The babies aren't killed by predators?"

"Of course not," Ezbai said again. "We have a spy planted in every village. This person notifies us whenever a baby is left to die. We come in and take it. Most of the so-called deformities are nothing our doctors can't fix in a trice."

"Thank goodness," said Chakotay. Paris had been right after all. They walked in silence for a while. Chakotay frowned as something stirred in his memory. He turned to look at the sharp profile of the expedition's nominal leader.

"Remilkansuur," he said slowly. "Is that a title or a family name?"

"Family name," Ezbai replied. "My title is Shamraa."

"Do you have a relative named Khala?"

Ezbai stopped dead in his tracks. "What do you know about Khala?"

"It's a long story, but briefly, she somehow got transported to a planet surface without knowing how it happened. A short while later, Ensign Paris and I were transported in the same manner. The process brought us here."

"She's alive? She's all right?" Ezbai reached to clutch at Chakotay's robes.

Chakotay smiled. "She was in very good hands when I last saw her. I imagine she's aboard my ship right now."

"Where is your ship? Oh, this is wonderful, wonderful! She vanished right before my eyes. It almost killed our parents. Come on, we've got to get back and hail your ship right away!" He broke into a trot, and his team followed suit.

"That's not going to be easy," said Chakotay. "I have no idea where this planet is in relationship to my vessel."

"We'll find out," said Ezbai gaily. "We'll find out."

Paris glanced at the grief-stricken faces turned toward him. "What happened? How did he die?"

Trima pushed her way through the small crowd that had begun to gather around Paris. Her face was flushed blue and stained with tears, but he had never seen her stand straighter. He realized all at once that with Matroci's death, Trima had become Sumar-ka's spiritual leader, and she was clearly ready to accept that responsibility.

"It appears to have been a chosen death."

"A suicide?" Paris was horrified. What had driven poor Matroci to kill himself?

"The windows were closed tightly. The room was filled with smoke from the Sacred Plant. This was how our previous Culil died, embracing the smoke as a way to reach the Crafters. I had not thought Matroci so ardent in his faith. I am pleased that I was wrong."

"Pleased? A man has just killed himself and you're pleased?" Paris couldn't believe what he was hearing.

Trima stiffened, and her sapphire-blue eyes flashed. "You insult us, Stranger. But I will forgive you. You have not been long among our people, you do not yet understand. I grieve for the loss of Matroci. But I am glad that he has gone straight to the Crafters."

Paris didn't like what he was hearing. He didn't like it at all. "What about Chakotay? You said he was missing, Soliss."

Soliss nodded. "It is very strange that he would disappear the same night that Matroci died."

For a second, Paris didn't understand what Soliss was saying. Then comprehension dawned, and with it anger. "You're not suggesting that Chakotay had anything to do with Matroci's death?"

Soliss did not answer.

"Come on, Soliss! You know what kind of man he is. He respects your customs. Besides, didn't Trima say Matroci had died of smoke inhalation?"

The unwavering gaze of the man who had nursed him and Chakotay back to health unnerved Paris. A second thought occurred to him.

"Soliss," he said slowly, "you don't think that I . . ."

"I do not know what to think," said Soliss at last. "My heart is heavy with grief, and my mind is clouded. But rest assured, your story will be verified, Paris."

"Good. Because it did happen."

Soliss again regarded him searchingly. Finally he sighed deeply. "Forgive my suspicions, but I fear with each day my ideals falter a bit more. Come. We will help you prepare for the farewell ceremony."

"What about Chakotay? He could be lost in the jungle."

"You tell us you survived a night alone in the jungle with two *iislaks* at your feet," Soliss said sharply. "Chakotay has all the knowledge you have. Today we are mourning the death of our Culil. Chakotay will return if he is alive . . . and if he wishes to."

Paris opened his mouth to ask what Soliss meant by that last remark, but something in the Minister's eyes caused the question to die in his throat.

No work would be done that day. As if the planet itself were in mourning, the bright skies clouded and by midafternoon there was rain. Soliss cursed the rain, for it would make the pyre on which Matroci's body would be sent to the Crafters that much more difficult to light and keep lit. Paris bathed and changed into fresh new clothes. He was surprised when Yurula, her eyes bloodshot from weeping, placed a beautiful scarf around his neck and then deliberately tore a hole in it.

"This represents Matroci's life, too soon ended," she said softly. "You will toss it on the pyre when it is your turn."

There was no sign of Chakotay. Paris badly wanted to organize a search party, but everyone was too caught up in the preparations for Matroci's farewell ceremony to assist him. And he wasn't about to wander out there alone again.

At one point, braving the drizzle, he ventured to the edge of the rain forest. Before him, green loomed, thick and threatening and almost impenetrable.

"Come on, Chakotay," he said softly. "Where are you?"

As the gray day turned into a gray evening, the rain finally stopped. It took hours for the pyre to become more than a sullen, smoldering pile of slimy branches, but finally it caught. The villagers fed it with precious kindling, dried out for use in their own personal cookfires. For the next few days, at least, there would be no cooked food or hot water until more branches had dried.

It was well into the night, and the creatures of the jungle were singing, when Matroci's body was brought out of Trima's hut. Paris stood silent, watching the slow procession by the flickering of several dozen torches.

Trima was in the lead, wearing the specially colored and styled robes of a Culil. Her long hair was bound behind her, and the combination of formal robes and plaited hair made her seem even more distant and cold. Her face showed no emotion. She strode forward slowly, regally, like a queen approaching her subjects.

Behind her, Soliss and Yurula bore the body of the dead Culil on a stretcher. He had been ritually bathed and his limbs positioned properly. Wordlessly, Soliss and Yurula placed the corpse on the pyre.

"We come to say farewell to Matroci, our beloved Culil," said Trima, her voice resonant. "He was young to be taken from us, but like the Culil before him, he was too good for this existence. And so the smoke of the Sacred Plant filled his lungs and burst his heart, taking him for its own."

In the light provided by a dozen flickering torches, Paris could see that Matroci's skin was several shades darker than it had been when he was alive. That was indeed consistent with what he remembered about asphyxiation. Carbon monoxide, what he assumed would be emitted from the smoke of the Sacred Plant, bound oxygen sites on hemoglobin and prevented oxygen from being absorbed. The blood and tissues of a human would be cherry red. Those of the Culilann would likely be a dark purplish-blue.

"His soul has gone already," Trima continued. "It has merged with the smoke of the Sacred Planet and flown to the Crafters. They have surely welcomed as gentle and wise a Culil as Matroci."

Paris heard muffled sobs. Everyone was trying hard to make Matroci's death seem like a good thing, but Tom had yet to attend a happy funeral.

"Though we are full of joy for Matroci's soul, we are permitted to be sorrowful for ourselves. For we will no longer have his wisdom and gentle good humor to guide us."

Paris regarded the new Culil and thought, *No, we won't. We'll only have you, Trima, and your icy ad-*

herence to the letter of the law. For no reason that he could name, his skin began to crawl.

"Now it is time to send Matroci's body to be with his spirit. As his soul wafted to the Crafters on the smoke from the Sacred Plant, so now we send his body after the same fashion." She turned and, taking the nearest torch, thrust it deep into the pyre. It sputtered, lighting only grudgingly. Wisps of smoke seeped out. It would be well into the morning before Matroci's body would be consumed, if then.

Trima then unwound a scarf similar to the one Paris wore about his throat. She held it up so that all might see the rent in it, then placed it on the body. Soliss imitated her.

Around the circle it went, until it was Paris's turn. He stepped forward and tugged at the scarf. He held it aloft in both hands, showing the rest of Sumar-ka the hole, then started to place it on Matroci's chest.

He paused. He was standing fairly close to the body. The pyre was hardly too hot for comfort and he wanted to place the scarf on the dead man, not just toss it. From this vantage point he had a clear view of Matroci's abdomen.

The robes the Culil wore had fallen away from the body slightly during the trip from the hut to the pyre. Tom could see very clearly a bright blue ring on the man's skin. Within the ring, the skin was paler. It looked like a bizarre birthmark, which was clearly what the Culilann had taken it for. But it was not.

Sweating suddenly, Tom let go of the scarf and stepped away. Winnif stepped forward with her own scarf, and the ritual continued around the circle.

His mind reeled with the knowledge. What he was looking at was the characteristic wound pattern produced by a weapon using directed energy of some sort. Matroci might indeed have died of asphyxiation, but before that, someone had placed a weapon over his heart and fired.

The Culil had not committed suicide. He had been murdered—murdered by someone who had the weapon with which to do it.

The Culilann did not have technology that advanced. Three options flooded into Tom's brain.

The Alilann had attacked last night, killed Matroci, and abducted Chakotay. With no one hearing anything? Hardly likely.

Someone in the Culilann was in actuality an Alilann spy. Paris glanced at the faces and dismissed that thought. The third option was the worst, and just as unlikely as the others—which was to say, just as valid.

A phaser could be reconfigured to leave just such a mark, and Chakotay was gone.

CHAPTER

18

NEELIX SANG TO HIMSELF AS HE CLEANED THE LAST few pots and pans. It had been a pleasant day. All of his dishes, including a few new recipes, had turned out wonderfully. People had had seconds and thirds of that dish he'd created for Harry Kim, the Szechwan *yruss*-and-broccoli. He was pleasantly tired, looking forward to storytime with Naomi Wildman, a nice hot bath, then bed.

He was surprised to hear the door hiss open at this hour, even more surprised to see a haggard-looking Khala enter. She took a few steps, then halted.

"Oh, I'm sorry," she said. "You're closing up." She turned as if to leave.

"Kitchen's always open for hungry bellies," said

Neelix. "Especially for you, because the replicator's available twenty-four hours a day. What can I get you?" He hastened over to the replicator and stood poised, ready to ask the computer to prepare his visitor whatever her stomach desired.

"That's just it," said Khala. "I don't want replicated food." She looked miserable, and the words came out slowly, reluctantly.

Neelix stared. "I'm sorry? You say you *don't* want replicator food?"

"Yes," she said in a whisper.

"You . . . you want me to cook something for you?"

She nodded. She looked as if she were about to be sick.

"Are you sure?" Neelix couldn't believe what he was hearing.

"Yes, I'm sure." She took a deep, shuddering breath and sat down at the counter. Khala sat erect, her hands folded in front of her. Neelix thought she looked like someone bracing herself for a painful interrogation session. "I want cooked food."

He wanted to pat her on the shoulder and reassure her it wouldn't be that bad. Some of his dishes weren't all that popular with the crew, but he had been chef aboard *Voyager* long enough to figure out what they liked. But for Khala, it probably would be pretty bad. He recalled her first experience with the tomato, how she had enjoyed the taste until she remembered what it was. He suspected they would be in for more of the same tonight.

Nonetheless, he was not about to turn down the request. He'd stay up all night if she wanted him to, the brave girl. He scurried back behind the counter, donning his apron and chef's hat with a sense of importance.

"What would you like, my dear?" he said very gently, patting her hand.

"I don't know."

"Well, what have you enjoyed in the past?"

Haltingly, she listed some of the foods she'd replicated and liked. Neelix was impressed with her range. Unfortunately, he did not have the materials for anything she cited on hand.

"Why don't we start with something simple," he said. "I'll make you a roast *yruss* sandwich."

She nodded glumly, resigned to her fate. He explained that he had baked the bread fresh that afternoon, that the spread was made from roasted mashed roots that the crew had reportedly found very tasty, that the meat was very similar to something called "beef," that the lettuce was grown in the aeroponics bay and had been picked only a few hours ago.

He might have been talking to himself. Khala was lost in thought, nodding slightly from time to time, sometimes at the wrong things. Neelix knew people too well to be offended by her lack of attention. Something was really troubling this poor girl.

He carefully cut the sandwich in two, poured a glass of ice water, and set the meal in front of her.

"*Bon appétit,*" he said.

She stared at the sandwich as if it were something that might bite back. Finally, she took a deep breath and picked up a half.

Neelix found himself leaning forward as Khala

brought the sandwich to her mouth, opened her blue lips, bit down, and chewed. With an effort, she swallowed.

And the bite came right back up.

She spat it into her napkin and began to cry. "I'm sorry, Neelix," she sobbed.

"Oh, honey," he soothed, rushing around the counter to hug her cautiously. "It's all right, you don't have to eat it if you don't want to."

"But I *do!*" she wailed, giving full vent to her heartache now. She leaned into Neelix's comforting arms. "I do! I have to learn to like grown food and . . . and art and music—I have to!"

"Now, now," said Neelix, patting her back awkwardly. "I'm sure that's not captain's orders."

She drew back, dabbing at her eyes with her napkin. She laughed shakily. "No, it's not. But it might just as well be."

Very gently, with great sympathy, Neelix said softly, "It's Ensign Kim, isn't it?"

She nodded. Fresh tears filled her eyes and trickled down her blue cheeks. "I hurt him so badly the other day. He played his clar—cluri—"

"Clarinet," Neelix supplied helpfully.

"For me. It's obvious he loves it, that this noise he makes means something to him. But Neelix, that's what the Culilann do. They play music, and they make things, and they eat food that comes right out of the ground or from animals they raise and then *kill*. It goes against everything I believe in, everything I've been raised to honor and admire. But Harry—have you ever been in love, Neelix?"

He thought of Kes. Her image appeared in his mind's eye, a tiny, perfectly formed girl with large blue eyes, golden hair, and a wisdom far beyond her years. He thought of her soft, husky voice, the exquisite gentleness of her manner. His heart contracted a little. It always would, regardless of the years since she had been among the *Voyager* crew. He would love her, after a fashion, for the rest of his life.

"Yes," he said simply. "I have."

"Then you know," said Khala. "You know how it feels. You know how much you want to do things with that person, to share interests, to take pleasure in the things that bring him or her pleasure."

He knew.

"And I can't do that. I can't. I'm trying, but look at this. I can't even eat a single bite of this sandwich."

Neelix opened his mouth to spout words of wisdom. He would tell her that just being herself was enough for Harry, that she didn't need to change just to please someone else. Usually, that was sound advice. But Khala wasn't trying to wipe out who she was, she was trying to expand herself. Trying to appreciate something another culture valued. He'd seen her with the tomato, he knew that once she could get over this irrational fear that she would enjoy the delights of fresh food, of music, of art.

"Let's try again," he said, and she brightened. "I think a simple broth, well watered down, would be a good start."

Captain's personal log, supplemental: After the unadulterated success we have achieved in cleans-

ing the Kwaisi ship of dark matter, we feel confident as we press on toward their homeworld. This will be the biggest and most important test of the Shepherd technology yet—attempting to engulf an entire planet. But I feel we are up to the task. I cannot begin to articulate how proud I am of our crew and our guest, Dr. R'Mor. He has been invaluable.

I am not as fond of our other guests, however. Ulaahn has become almost unbearable. I am pleased that we have been able to help his people, but I must confess, I will not be at all sorry to move on.

The door to her ready room hissed open. Tuvok stood in the doorway, hands behind his back. "Captain, we are about to enter the Kwaisi home system."

"Wonderful," said Janeway, and meant it. She hastened onto the bridge. Ulaahn, predictably, was already there, pacing unhappily. He whirled as she entered.

"Captain! What have you been doing hiding in your ready room? This is dire!"

That did it. "Captain Ulaahn, you and your people have been shown every courtesy aboard this vessel. We have devoted this ship and its crew to helping you. We have now come to help your entire planet. A thank you may be too much to expect, I realize that, but you will cease berating me on my own bridge. Is that understood?"

He scowled and did not answer. Janeway would accept silence. She nodded and slipped into her chair, calling up her console with a quick touch of her left hand.

"Torres, report."

"There's a lot of dark matter in this system," came her chief engineer's voice. "With Dr. R'Mor's help, we were able to ascertain that this was where one of his wormholes opened. The concentration is greatest around that area and diminishes as it's spread forth."

"That should be our top priority."

"Already on it," said Torres. "That was the first thing we figured out how to do. It's child's play to us now."

Janeway's heart swelled with pride. She remembered that first tentative transport of a smattering of dark-matter particles. They had gone from not having the slightest idea as to what the floating orb Tialin had given them did to creating their own warp-bubble universe to exploring the radiation sphere that would enable them to cleanse whole moons and planets.

I don't know what the extent of your powers are, Tialin, she thought, *but I hope that somehow you can see just how damn good a job we're doing.*

"Then play, Torres," she said, and let the smile grow on her lips.

They made their way through the system. The central star, fortunately, did not seem to be home to any pieces of mutated dark matter. It was all in the single planet, the Kwaisi homeworld. And there seemed to be a lot of it.

"Mr. Tuvok, report."

"Our guest appears to be telling the truth about his seven ships being his planet's only defensive vessels," said Tuvok.

"Of course I—" Ulaahn began, but Janeway shut him up with a look.

"I detect no vessels other than small transport ships in orbit around the planet. It appears safe to continue our approach."

It was time to pour some oil on the water. "Captain," said Janeway, turning to Ulaahn, "you said your planet is infected with the dark matter, that people are behaving irrationally. Will they listen to us—to you?"

Ulaahn seemed about to make an angry retort, but with an effort he calmed himself. "I do not know, Captain. The dark matter appears to affect people differently. Some in my crew turned hostile. I, as you know, was suicidal." He said the last word in a deep, disapproving grumble. Though Janeway clearly remembered his depression, it was hard to imagine the alien before her ever doubting himself.

"In order to operate the sphere to purge the planet, we'll have to take our warp engines off-line and lower our shields," she reminded him. "We'll be very vulnerable. I've no intention of approaching your planet in such a fashion until I can speak to someone and be reassured that we won't be in any danger."

With evident reluctance, Ulaahn told her about the weapons on his homeworld. There weren't many. The Kwaisi did indeed seem to rely on the eight— seven, now—heavily armed vessels under Ulaahn's command to protect them.

Still, better safe than sorry. "Go to Yellow Alert. Shields up. Mr. Kim, please open a hailing frequency." At Kim's nod, she continued. "This is Captain Kathryn Janeway of the Federation *Starship Voyager,* to the Kwaisi Council. You will have noticed that we come escorted by seven of your defensive vessels. With me on my bridge is Captain Ulaahn, commander of that fleet. We come to help you. We wish to warn you about a danger to your planet and people of which you are more than likely unaware. It is directly responsible for any chaos that has occurred on your homeworld."

"No answer, Captain," said Kim.

"Captain Ulaahn, why don't you try?" asked Janeway.

Ulaahn straightened in Chakotay's chair and cleared his throat. "This is Captain Ulaahn, to the Council. What this Janeway says is the truth. They have technology that can save all of us." He paused. "Ensign, is that frequency open?"

"Yes, sir," replied Kim. "They are receiving. They just aren't responding."

Ulaahn nodded, then seemed to reach a decision. He rose, speaking as if to someone who was present. "Eriih, my old friend, you must listen to me. We have been infected with something that makes us mad and attacks our bodies. I personally was so distraught and affected by this that I opened fire on one of my own vessels." His voice caught. "I will of course stand trial for my crime."

Janeway stared. They would be able to show that Ulaahn had not been of sound mind when he ordered the destruction of one of his own ships, but why even bother? She was certain that thousands, if not hundreds of thousands, of people had committed comparable crimes. If every one of them had to undergo trial, this whole planet could be tied up in litigation for years.

"Please answer us. Let me help my people."

There was a long silence. It seemed that Ulaahn's moving plea had fallen on deaf ears. Then the screen came to life. An elderly man with haunted eyes locked gazes with Ulaahn.

"Flee, my young friend," said the man, whom Janeway presumed was Eriih. "You would not want to see what has become of the Kwaisi. The Council has been overthrown, terror rules the streets. There have been mass suicides. Weapons have been stolen and aimed not at enemies but at friends. Find a world that will welcome you, not this rock of hatred."

"We can cure your people," said Janeway, rising and stepping down to the viewscreen. "All we ask is assurance that you do not attack us."

"I cannot give such an assurance," replied Eriih. "Whatever it is you intend to do to us, it cannot be worse than what we have done to ourselves." He pressed a button on the console in front of him, and the screen was once again filled with stars.

"How much longer until we reach orbit?" asked Janeway.

"Eighteen minutes, twenty-two seconds," replied Tuvok.

"Senior staff to ready room. Now."

The meeting was of necessity brief. Janeway filled her staff in on the exchange with Eriih. "There are no assurances that whatever weapons are on the planet won't be trained on us," she finished.

"There are not many weapons that could threaten this ship on the face of the planet," said Ulaahn. "And from the sound of things, most of them have been trained on other targets. Kwaisi targets," he said bitterly.

"Torres? The planet can wait. It's the people who are posing the threat, and who need to be healed the fastest."

"We don't need to actually beam anyone aboard this ship," Torres pointed out. "All we need to do in order to remove the dark matter is dematerialize them and separate it out. We can do that right on the planet without taking them anywhere. We can accommodate more people if we take certain computer functions off-line and use those terabytes to increase the size of the transport buffer."

"How many at a time?" asked Janeway.

Torres thought. "Probably up to two hundred, two twenty at a go. As I say, it will mean shutting down certain computer operations. It is not without risk."

"How risky?"

"If you'd asked me a month ago, I'd have said the risk was high. Now? Minimal. We've gambled so much in the last few days, Captain, that I think we finally know what we're dealing with."

Janeway considered all the information, then put her hands down on the table. "Let's do it."

CHAPTER
19

"ENTERING ORBIT AROUND THE KWAISI HOMEWORLD,"
stated Tuvok. "There is no sign of aggression from
the planet."

"Red Alert." The bridge darkened and the too-
familiar red pulse began. "Torres, you may begin shutting down all nonessential computer operations. Get
that pattern buffer as large as you can make it. Kim,
monitor all signals from the planet. I want to hear the
Kwaisi reactions, if any, to what we're about to do."

Kim swallowed. Janeway knew she was asking
him to juggle more balls in the air than he had ever
attempted before. Gamely, he replied, "Aye, Captain."

"Ulaahn, do you have a suggestion as to where we
should begin?"

He was staring at the image of his planet in the viewscreen. Janeway had to repeat her question. He jumped, as if startled out of a deep reverie.

"Takna-Marr is the capital city," Ulaahn said. "It has the largest population. It's also where the most weapons are located. I would begin there."

"We're starting with the capital city of Takna-Marr," Torres told her team. Seven entered the coordinates.

"The population is four hundred twenty-two thousand," said Seven. She raised a golden eyebrow. "This may take some time."

"We need to identify and focus on those individuals in whom the concentration of dark matter is greatest," Telek reminded them.

"That, too, may take some time," said Seven.

It did, but not as much time as they had feared. They divided the city into square-kilometer portions and scanned those areas individually. They found only ten thousand two hundred twelve who had any concentration of dark matter at all, and of those, four hundred two registered dangerously high levels.

"Let's get them," said Torres. "Engineering to bridge. We've targeted four hundred people in the capital who are the sickest or who will likely pose the greatest threat. We're ready to begin when you are."

"The shields are down," said the captain. "Do it."

"Energize," Torres said, and crossed her fingers.

The transporter did not explode. The warp-core bubble did not burst. The extra terabytes provided by shutting down all nonessential computer activity enabled them to successfully dematerialize the first two hundred without any problem. If only that awful noise and light would stop, Torres might begin to think of this task as a cakewalk.

"Get the next batch," she ordered.

Again, they dematerialized two hundred people, separated out the lethal mutated dark matter, and rematerialized them. And again, everything seemed to be all right.

"We were successful on our end, Captain. Awaiting your orders."

"Harry, any reaction?" asked Janeway.

For a moment, Kim didn't reply. "There's a lot going on. I've been following one signal that's been broadcasting every known instance of violence in the capital. They're saying that suddenly, in the midst of a street brawl, people shimmered out of existence and then reappeared."

"And?" Try as she might, Janeway couldn't keep the excitement out of her voice.

"And when they returned, they were horrified at what they'd done. The wounded are being cared for by the same people who inflicted the injuries." His face shone with delight. "It's working, Captain!"

"Tuvok?"

"Still no sign of aggression from the planet directed at us," Tuvok reported.

"Excellent. B'Elanna, continue."

There were fewer infected with the dark matter than Torres had feared. In groups of two hundred at a time, they located those whose tissue was inundated by the dark matter and freed them from the infection. Bit by bit, person by person, the Kwaisi returned to their normal selves.

Torres didn't let herself get too carried away. Their plan might be working—all right, so it was working perfectly—but there were still so many dead, so much damaged. For not the first time, she wondered what the enigmatic Tialin was keeping from them. Certainly, the rogue Shepherd she had mentioned, Lhiau, was a danger. But why? What did he want? What was it Tialin had told the away team? "Far, far more is at stake than I am permitted to tell you." Torres had been so caught up in figuring out how to unlock the orb's mysteries that she had forgotten about the bigger picture. Well, that big picture was right below their orbiting ship. People were dying, were killing, because of Lhiau, and once this was over Torres was going to get some answers.

The process was a time-consuming one, as Seven had predicted. But the more people they cured of the dark matter contamination, the easier it became. The Kwaisi started working with them, instead of running madly in the streets. Janeway was able to establish contact with the Council, who had, by this time, returned to their former official building. They were able to negotiate shutting down the few weapons that would pose any threat. The replicators were put to work making blankets, clothing, and medical supplies. So as not to interfere with the transport of infected persons, all the shuttlecrafts, loaded with supplies, went to the surface.

Neelix sent little Naomi Wildman down to engineering with a tray of sandwiches and coffee. The nearly exhausted team partook eagerly. Torres noticed that Khala hesitated only briefly before taking her own sandwich; she did not inquire if it had been replicated.

They took breaks in shifts, calling in Carey, Vorrik, and others in engineering to take over for fifteen minutes at a stretch. Finally, hours later, it was done. Everyone on the planet surface who had been infected with dark matter had been cleansed of it.

"Well done, Torres," said Janeway. "How about nonhumanoid life forms that have been infected?"

"Seven has the numbers on that. We can do it the same way we did the Kwaisi. It's a lot, but not more than we can handle."

"Excellent. Since you already know how to do that, we'll save that for last."

Torres knew what Janeway was going to order next. The final test of their knowledge of Shepherd technology: expanding the radiation emitted by the purple sphere to surround the entire planet.

"We're as ready as we'll ever be," she said.

"Then do it."

Torres and her team went about taking the warp core off-line. Now, they had neither warp drive nor shields. She was glad that these people were friendly. No shields, no warp drive—they were sitting ducks. Once they had the warp core off-line, Torres nodded to R'Mor.

The Romulan tapped in the command on the console. At once, the orb began screeching and glowing. Amid the light and the noise, Seven called out what was happening.

"The radiation sphere is increasing. It is closing the distance between us and the planet. It has reached the planet. It is continuing to grow at an exponential rate. It has completely engulfed the—"

Her voice sounded loud in the sudden stillness. She broke off in mid-sentence. The sphere was hovering peacefully, purple instead of red, its task done. It had taken only seventeen seconds to gather up all the dark matter that had been embedded in the planet's soil and lower life-forms, not to mention every piece of Kwaisi machinery. It was incredible.

"The amount of dark matter in the warp bubble has increased by six thousand four hundred percent," reported Seven.

And smiled.

Janeway was tired. She hadn't realized how on edge she had been these last several days, as Torres, R'Mor, and their crew pushed through the barriers of ignorance one by one to reach this moment of exhausted victory. So when Eriih insisted on a conference, she desperately wanted to beg off.

"It is a rare honor," Ulaahn exclaimed. "You cannot refuse!"

"I can and will," bridled Janeway.

Ulaahn raised his hands in a pleading gesture. "Perhaps I should say, I would urge you to accept. It would mean a great deal to my people to thank you in person. Perhaps you could postpone the meeting. That would give Eriih a chance to organize a formal dinner to thank you for your assistance."

A lengthy formal dinner with a tableful of Kwaisi

was the absolute last thing Janeway wanted at this point. "All right," she said tiredly. "I will meet with your Council now and get it over with."

Tuvok, the epitome of caution as ever, insisted that a security guard accompany his captain when she beamed down. He would not be overruled, no matter how much Ulaahn protested. It was therefore three people who materialized in the shambles that had once been the Council Chamber a few hours later.

Janeway could not help but be saddened and angered anew at the destruction caused by the mutated dark matter. This had once been a beautiful building. Murals had been painted on the walls; fine carpets covered the floor. Now, the carpets had been slashed, and the walls had huge cracks and what looked like graffiti painted on them.

"Captain Janeway," said Eriih warmly. "You are the hero of our people. Please excuse the state of our hall. I think you already know the reason for it."

"I do indeed, and I am grateful that there was not further damage or loss of life." Janeway permitted herself to be guided gently into a chair and accepted a glass of cherry-red liquor. It smelled terrible and tasted even worse, but she managed a small swallow in the name of courtesy. She gave the other six members of the Council, who sat at the dusty table with her, a strained smile.

"Your intervention was responsible for the fact that there was no further damage or loss of life," said Eriih generously. He took a healthy swallow of the beverage. "Ulaahn. Welcome home. You understand that after these formalities . . ." His voice trailed off. He looked uncomfortable.

"I do," said Ulaahn staunchly. "I feel certain that I will be exonerated, but I will stand trial."

Janeway glanced from one to the other, slightly disturbed by the conversation. Despite her dislike of Ulaahn, she felt compelled to defend what he had done and tried to do.

"Eriih, may I say that Ulaahn cannot be held responsible for his actions, any more than you or the vandal in the street who attacked his neighbor. The dark matter rendered everyone affected temporarily insane, if it didn't attack them physically."

"Yes, the dark matter," said Eriih, deftly changing the subject. "We know of dark matter, Captain. Our scientists theorize that it is quite harmless. Please, if you have learned anything that may protect us in the future, we would be grateful to learn it."

"Dark matter *is* harmless in its natural state," said Janeway. A servant refilled her glass. She did not take another sip. "But the dark matter you encountered had been mutated, rendered dangerous."

"How?"

Janeway sighed. It had become abundantly clear to her that these people were litigious, orderly, detail-obsessed, and autocratic. She did not think that they would willingly let her go until they understood everything, down to the last detail. So, gritting her teeth, she explained everything as quickly as possible. She told them of the pursuit by the Romulans, of Telek's wormholes and their unwitting abduction of him. She spoke of the disasters her own ship had faced, of locating Tialin, of the quest she had accepted to help remove all the mutated dark matter from the quadrant. She told of what the dark-matter cloaks had done to the Romulan warbirds, and how they had all worked together to decipher the purple sphere's mysteries.

"This Telek R'Mor—he is on your ship now? And he is the one who released this dark matter into the Delta Quadrant while he searched for your vessel?"

Janeway nodded. Then she realized why Eriih was asking the question. "Dr. R'Mor was forced to release the dark matter. He had no choice. His family was being held hostage," she said, perhaps too quickly. "Also, he had no idea at the time that the wormholes were releasing anything dangerous. It's largely because of him that we were able to utilize the Shepherd technology to save your world. You ought to be grateful to him."

"Oh, we are, we are. And to you, Captain." Eriih saluted her with his glass while the rest of the Council nodded their agreement. "And such evidence will no doubt exonerate your Romulan friend."

Janeway sat up straighter in her chair. "Exonerate?"

"Certainly. He released this terrible plague upon us, unwittingly or no. That he volunteered to correct his error will stand him in good stead at his trial."

Her eyes went icy. "There will be no trial of Dr. R'Mor. You have seen what this mutated dark matter can do. There are dozens of systems just like yours, infected and destroying themselves right this minute.

We have to go and help them. Surely you understand that!"

Eriih chuckled. "I'm not asking you to stay, Captain. Just release the doctor to us and you can be on your way."

"I can't do that. We need Dr. R'mor's knowledge and skill. Besides, he has more than atoned for—"

"That will be for a court to decide!" interrupted Ulaahn. "Dr. R'Mor committed a terrible crime against the Kwaisi. He must be tried by us!"

"I have had enough of this," said Janeway. She rose. The security guard behind her stepped backward. "We prevent Ulaahn from blowing up his entire fleet of ships and, incidentally, from killing hundreds of people, including himself. We work without ceasing to find a way to help your people and dozens more races just like yours. We come to your planet, render ourselves vulnerable in order to save your world, and you thank us by demanding that we turn over a skilled, remorseful scientist who will do far more good saving other people than languishing in a Kwaisi jail."

Eriih was frowning, but she didn't care. She pressed on.

"I have no wish to be rude, but it seems to me that R'Mor has done more than enough to help those he injured. Thank you for your hospitality, but we must be on our way." She touched her combadge. "Janeway to *Voyager*. Two to beam up."

Nothing happened. She touched the badge again. No responding chirp. It was dead.

"I'm sorry, Captain," said Eriih, "but your communications device and your weapons have been neutralized. A necessary precaution."

He gestured, and seven burly, well-armed soldiers stepped forward. "It is noble of you. I admire your willingness to sacrifice. Since you will not yield up Telek R'Mor, I have no choice but to take you, his captain, in his stead. Your captivity will not be harsh, Captain Janeway. We are not barbarians. You will be made comfortable as you await your trial."

"How long will that be?" Janeway demanded.

Eriih shrugged. "With so many to try, who can say? You are the last offender on the list right now, so it may take quite a while. A year or two, at the very least." He leaned forward conspiratorially. "But since your time is so precious, and we do appreciate what is at stake, we'll see what we can do to nudge it along, hmmm?"

The purple ball sparked to life.

"What the— Seven, R'Mor, what's going on?" demanded Torres. They were about to quit for the night and spend an hour winding down together at the Polynesian resort, when That Damned Ball started glowing.

"Unknown," said Seven.

"Do not worry," came the voice of Tialin the Shepherd, soft and melodious. The ball pulsated in time to the words. "Nothing is wrong. I am just taking a moment to congratulate you on your progress.

"If you are hearing this message, that means that you have learned how to utilize the orb I gave you. You have conducted experiments and called forth courage to face the unknown. You have learned how to gather the dark matter from space, from inanimate objects, from lower life-forms, from humanoids, even from a planet-sized object. You have understood the purpose of the sphere and have created your own safe place for the dark matter to reside until it is time for me to retrieve it. You have done well, very well. Had you not been able to figure this out on your own, you would not have been up to the task I set you in other ways either, and you would have been unfit custodians for so dangerous and volatile a thing as mutated dark matter."

"So this was a test?" said Torres. "Of all the—"

"Telek R'Mor," continued Tialin, "I have more information, for your ears alone. It was you who were technically responsible for the dark matter being unleashed on this system, though I know it was not your will. Listen, and decide if your comrades can bear the hearing of this news."

Telek stared raptly at the ball. Torres couldn't hear anything, but clearly Telek could. His eyes widened and his face paled.

"No," he whispered. "That's not possible. It cannot be, it cannot!"

The orb continued speaking silently to Telek, until finally it darkened. As if released from its grip physically as well as mentally, Telek staggered. Khala was there, gently propping him up.

"Telek?" said Torres. "What did it tell you?"

He licked his lips. There was fear on his face. "Something amazing—something terrible beyond imagining. I thought, in my dealings with the Tal

Shiar, that I had some notion of what evil is. But I was innocent of the true depths of it until this moment. Lhiau must be stopped. He must! It all depends on it!"

"What?" cried Torres, exasperated.

"Everything!" It made no sense, and Torres opened her mouth to try again. But R'Mor was already heading for the turbolift and the bridge.

Telek leaned against the wall of the turbolift. "Bridge," he told it. Frantically, Telek sought to gather his thoughts.

More was at stake than he could begin to articulate. Tialin had given him the knowledge, but he was free to share it if he felt it was the wise thing to do. He needed to talk to Janeway. She was a fellow scientist at heart; she would understand. And she could help him decide if this was something that the whole crew needed to know, or just the two of them.

Telek almost stumbled out of the turbolift in his haste. "Captain," he gasped, but her chair was empty. "Commander Tuvok, where is the Captain?"

Tuvok did not look up from his console. "Dr. R'Mor, I suggest you return to engineering or your quarters. The bridge is no place for you at this time."

"Why not? What's going on? Where is Captain Janeway?" Now he saw how tense everyone on the bridge was, even Tuvok, in his Vulcan way.

Tuvok looked up, his brown eyes meeting Telek's.

"Captain Janeway has been kidnapped."

EPILOGUE

IT WAS BITTERLY COLD IN THE TINY CELL, AND IT stank. This was something Jekri had never before experienced. Her dealings with her prisoners ended once they had been sentenced. If she needed them afterward, she sent for them. She had never even seen a Romulan holding cell.

With macabre humor she mused that she should probably enjoy the experience. Soon enough, they would probably take her and interrogate her, and she knew what *that* meant well enough.

They had confiscated all her philotostan chips. She had not had the chance to have one embedded in a false tooth, as the more fortunate Sharibor had. No, they had stripped her naked, poked and probed her, removed all the chips she had secreted in her clothing and on her person, then flung these filthy rags at her and ushered her into this cell.

She sank down and huddled in a corner, drawing her knees up to her chest. For a brief instant, Jekri indulged in self-pity. She had been so high, so proud, once, and now she was dung on the boot of the Empress. She did not deserve this. She deserved respect. She had earned it with blood and loyalty, but they had ripped all dignity away from her. She supposed she could consider herself lucky they had not placed her with other prisoners. There were many who were here because of Jekri's orders, and they would not be gentle once they saw her.

The chairman of the Tal Shiar would have died in the service of the Empire. She would have killed herself rather than face such disgrace as Jekri was now enduring. But at that farce of a trial, Lhiau and his cronies had ripped away all remnants of that august office from one Jekri Kaleh. She was no longer chairman of the Tal Shiar. She was nothing, no one, a corpse that had the temerity to still be alive.

She lifted her head from her knees. No. She was *not* nothing.

The chairman was dead, and with that death came an end to any loyalty she had to the rulers of the Empire. They had betrayed her. She owed them nothing now, not the Empress, not the Praetor or Proconsul, certainly not Verrak, who had wounded her more deeply than she would have guessed. She was her own person now, and she would be damned if she walked docilely to her execution.

She had to escape. And once free, there was only one thing she could do that would make the Empress again regard her with the honor that was her due. In order to resurrect the chairman, Jekri had to become the Little Dagger again, the thief and killer and stalker in the shadows.

It was a bitter draft. It was irony of the highest sort.

And it was the only logical thing to do.

About the Author

Christie Golden is the author of thirteen novels and fourteen short stories. Among her credits are three other *Voyager* novels—*The Murdered Sun, Marooned,* and *Seven of Nine*—as well as a Tom Paris short story, "A Night at Sandrine's," for *Amazing Stories.* On the strength of *The Murdered Sun,* Golden now has an open invitation to pitch for *Voyager,* the show.

In addition to *Star Trek* novels, Golden has also written three original fantasy novels, *Instrument of Fate, King's Man and Thief,* and, under the pen name Jadrien Bell, *A.D. 999.*

Golden lives in Colorado with her husband, two cats, and a white German shepherd. Readers are encouraged to visit her Web site at www.sff.net/people/Christie.Golden.

Look for STAR TREK fiction from Pocket Books

Star Trek®: The Original Series

Enterprise: The First Adventure • Vonda N. McIntyre
Final Frontier • Diane Carey
Strangers from the Sky • Margaret Wander Bonanno
Spock's World • Diane Duane
The Lost Years • J.M. Dillard
Probe • Margaret Wander Bonanno
Prime Directive • Judith and Garfield Reeves-Stevens
Best Destiny • Diane Carey
Shadows on the Sun • Michael Jan Friedman
Sarek • A.C. Crispin
Federation • Judith and Garfield Reeves-Stevens
Vulcan's Forge • Josepha Sherman & Susan Shwartz
Mission to Horatius • Mack Reynolds
Vulcan's Heart • Josepha Sherman & Susan Shwartz

Novelizations
Star Trek: The Motion Picture • Gene Roddenberry
Star Trek II: The Wrath of Khan • Vonda N. McIntyre
Star Trek III: The Search for Spock • Vonda N. McIntyre
Star Trek IV: The Voyage Home • Vonda N. McIntyre
Star Trek V: The Final Frontier • J.M. Dillard
Star Trek VI: The Undiscovered Country • J.M. Dillard
Star Trek Generations • J.M. Dillard
Starfleet Academy • Diane Carey

Star Trek books by William Shatner with Judith and Garfield
Reeves-Stevens
The Ashes of Eden
The Return
Avenger
Star Trek: Odyssey (contains *The Ashes of Eden*, *The Return*, and
   Avenger)
Spectre
Dark Victory

#1 • *Star Trek: The Motion Picture* • Gene Roddenberry
#2 • *The Entropy Effect* • Vonda N. McIntyre
#3 • *The Klingon Gambit* • Robert E. Vardeman
#4 • *The Covenant of the Crown* • Howard Weinstein
#5 • *The Prometheus Design* • Sondra Marshak & Myrna Culbreath

Star Trek: The Next Generation®

Star Trek: Voyager®

#17 • *Death of a Neutron Star* • Eric Kotani
#18 • *Battle Lines* • Dave Galanter & Greg Brodeur
#19-21 • *Dark Matters* • Christie Golden
   #19 • *Cloak and Dagger*
   #20 • *Ghost Dance*
   #21 • *Shadow of Heaven*

Star Trek®: New Frontier

New Frontier #1-4 Collector's Edition • Peter David
#1 • *House of Cards* • Peter David
#2 • *Into the Void* • Peter David
#3 • *The Two-Front War* • Peter David
#4 • *End Game* • Peter David
#5 • *Martyr* • Peter David
#6 • *Fire on High* • Peter David
The Captain's Table #5 • *Once Burned* • Peter David
Double Helix #5 • *Double or Nothing* • Peter David
#7 • *The Quiet Place* • Peter David
#8 • *Dark Allies* • Peter David
#9-11 • *Excalibur* • Peter David
   #9 • *Requiem*
   #10 • *Renaissance*
   #11 • *Restoration*

Star Trek®: Invasion!

#1 • *First Strike* • Diane Carey
#2 • *The Soldiers of Fear* • Dean Wesley Smith & Kristine Kathryn Rusch
#3 • *Time's Enemy* • L.A. Graf
#4 • *Final Fury* • Dafydd ab Hugh
Invasion! Omnibus • various

Star Trek®: Day of Honor

#1 • *Ancient Blood* • Diane Carey
#2 • *Armageddon Sky* • L.A. Graf
#3 • *Her Klingon Soul* • Michael Jan Friedman
#4 • *Treaty's Law* • Dean Wesley Smith & Kristine Kathryn Rusch
The Television Episode • Michael Jan Friedman
Day of Honor Omnibus • various

Star Trek®: The Captain's Table

#1 • *War Dragons* • L.A. Graf
#2 • *Dujonian's Hoard* • Michael Jan Friedman
#3 • *The Mist* • Dean Wesley Smith & Kristine Kathryn Rusch
#4 • *Fire Ship* • Diane Carey
#5 • *Once Burned* • Peter David
#6 • *Where Sea Meets Sky* • Jerry Oltion

Star Trek®: The Dominion War

#1 • *Behind Enemy Lines* • John Vornholt
#2 • *Call to Arms...* • Diane Carey
#3 • *Tunnel Through the Stars* • John Vornholt
#4 • *...Sacrifice of Angels* • Diane Carey

Star Trek®: The Badlands

#1 • Susan Wright
#2 • Susan Wright

Star Trek® Books available in Trade Paperback

Omnibus Editions
    Invasion! Omnibus • various
    Day of Honor Omnibus • various
    The Captain's Table Omnibus • various
    Star Trek: Odyssey • William Shatner with Judith and Garfield
      Reeves-Stevens
Other Books
    Legends of the Ferengi • Ira Steven Behr & Robert Hewitt Wolfe
    Strange New Worlds, vols. I, II, and III • Dean Wesley Smith, ed.
    Adventures in Time and Space • Mary Taylor
    The Lives of Dax • Marco Palmieri, ed.
    Captain Proton! • Dean Wesley Smith
    The Klingon Hamlet • Wil'yam Shex'pir
    New Worlds, New Civilizations • Michael Jan Friedman
    Enterprise Logs • Carol Greenburg, ed.

STAR TREK
THE EXPERIENCE
LAS VEGAS HILTON

Be a part of the most exciting deep space adventure in the galaxy as you beam aboard the U.S.S. Enterprise. Explore the evolution of Star Trek® from television to movies in the "History of the Future Museum," the planet's largest collection of authentic Star Trek memorabilia. Then, visit distant galaxies on the "Voyage Through Space." This 22-minute action packed adventure will capture your senses with the latest in motion simulator technology. After your mission, shop in the Deep Space Nine Promenade and enjoy 24th Century cuisine in Quark's Bar & Restaurant.

Save up to $30

CODE:1007a   EXPIRES 12/31/00

HAPPY HOLIDAYS
FROM NEELIX AND

KOMAR COOKIES from the STAR TREK COOKBOOK

When I was courting Kes, I was a lot leaner—in fact I spent a few years as a swimsuit model on Talax—but now I've filled out, and why not? I always say, "Beware the skinny cook." One of the reasons I've gained a little weight is this dish created by the Komar. They live in a nebula and feed off the neural energy of other species. They're not real nice, but they make a great cookie. They don't bake theirs—they zap the dough with a magnetodynamic TL 5 solar-photox blast, but you don't have to do that, unless you know how. The dough is made from rattle fern caviar, Turian stardust, and Betelgeuse butter. The Komar also add wineworm blood, but I think this detracts from the already intense taste. ADAPTED FOR 20th CENTURY KITCHENS

1 cup all purpose flour
1/2 cup (1 stick) of butter
1/2 cup light brown sugar
1 egg

1 egg white
1 tsp. cinnamon
1/2 tsp. vanilla extract
1/4 tsp. salt

granulated sugar, as needed for coating
raspberry or strawberry jelly or preserves

THE STAR TREK® COOKBOOK
The official cookbook from <u>Star Trek</u>'s first chef!

HAPPY HOLIDAYS
FROM NEELIX AND

Cream the butter and brown sugar and beat in the whole egg, flour, vanilla, cinnamon, and salt. Roll the dough and chill in your refrigerator for about 15 minutes while you preheat your oven to 375 degrees. When the dough has been chilled, break off individual 1-inch pieces and roll into small balls. Lightly beat egg white in a small bowl until it's slightly frothy, not membranous. Next, fill a small bowl with granulated sugar. Coat the balls in the egg white and then roll them in sugar to coat them. Now arrange them on a flat greased baking sheet and make a slight impression in each with your finger—or you can use the broad end of a chopstick or even a thimble. Drop a small amount of raspberry or strawberry jelly or preserves into each depression and close over the depression with the cookie dough. Bake at 375 degrees for about 10 minutes. Allow to cool before serving.

These make incredible Christmas and holiday gifts and can become a holiday tradition. Wrap them in fancy paper and bows for friends and neighbors. Yields two dozen cookies.

THE STAR TREK®COOKBOOK
Star Trek cuisine for the earthbound chef!